THE WIDOW'S CLOAK

A RUSSELL FAMILY NOVELLA

LYNNE BASHAM TAGAWA

Blue Rock Press

For all the Marys

CHAPTER 1

*C*ulloden moor fell silent, but the echo of cannon lingered in Iain MacLeod's ears. Only the occasional crack of muskets disturbed the quiet.

Iain fought to see the results of the battle through the stand of birch and willow, but smoke cast a pall over the winter-browned expanse beyond.

Was his father beyond the smoke?

He pressed through the willow saplings to get a better view of the moor. An acrid smell reached him, underlaid by a tinge of something worse. Red flashed once through the haze. The MacDonalds's tartan, or perhaps the Frasers's. The MacLeod green did not appear.

They'd followed the prince to victory at Prestonpans, but this day smelled of loss. They were brave but outnumbered. And outgunned. Iain's fist clenched. He'd nearly reached his father's height and had some knowledge of the sword and

1

targe. He could have joined the rest of the clan in battle. He drew a long breath. He had his own task in this fight against the German usurper.

Last fall, his father had asked him to care for the clan's oxen and horses when they mustered to fight. And he'd done so over the long months of rough living, watching as provisions for man and beast grew shorter and shorter.

The mare nickered. Iain turned and made his way back, the boggy ground sucking at the thin soles of his shoes.

"Dinna fret," he crooned, pulling up her picket and leading her to another spot. The laird's mare was thin, her chestnut coat rough, but she had survived this far. With fresh new grass she might yet make it home, unlike her stable mate. He found a place that looked promising, where tender April shoots winked beneath the dead bracken. Then he guided the gaunt oxen to a new spot, an easy task, as they had no energy to fight him.

The laird's men, one hundred all told, now possessed only a single baggage wagon with almost nothing left inside. For three weeks they'd had little to eat, except—

Iain's mind shied away from the death of the gelding. The others had been unanimous that the meat should not be given to the circling corbies. One of the men had given him a bit of bannock in exchange for his portion of the horseflesh.

Somewhere nearby, a skylark chittered, oblivious to the dying embers of the battle.

His father—

Nausea assailed Iain's belly as he imagined his father, one of the laird's right-hand men, in the front lines, facing cannon fire. Well, it was over now, or almost. How many would come back?

More musket fire, a few pops and cracks. A scream. The bird stopped singing.

Iain went back for another look at the battlefield. Navigating the wet ground, he thought of the laird's appearance when he'd returned from a meeting the night before. Stark lines in his face made the man look ancient. Like he wore the mask of death. Had he foreseen this day's result?

Iain shoved aside a clinging willow branch. Something moved on the moor.

They were coming back. Some had survived the battle.

One, two, three. Two more behind them.

But none was his father.

No—where was he? Lying injured, in pain? He couldn't be dead.

Iain bolted past the last man and ignored their shouts to return.

* * *

IAIN GROANED IN THE DARKNESS. Pain lanced through his head as he fought to see.

Where was he?

He thrust out his hands, trying to lever himself up, but he only succeeded in driving a shaft of pain into his skull. He subsided, gasping.

"Lad?" A voice croaked nearby. "Dinna trouble yourself, ye took a mighty blow to the head. Rest yourself now."

Blow to the head? Broken images crowded in. Smoke above Culloden moor, the bodies—and worse, the men who lay gasping in their death throes. The stench of emptied bowels, the smell of blood copper in his mouth. Red-coated soldiers lifting and thrusting their muskets, bayonets red with blood. An occasional pistol shot.

He'd been searching for his father's form, always searching ... and finding cover when redcoats appeared.

3

He'd ducked behind piles of bodies when he couldn't find a wee hillock to hide behind. Cumberland's men must have found him, captured him, but the memory eluded him—

He knew only that he hadn't found his father.

"Drink, lad." The voice was closer.

Iain finally managed a half-sitting position. He could just make out a shadowy form and the ladle of water held before him. "Thank ye," he managed, and sipped.

A raging thirst seized him, and he made short work of the contents.

"Wait a few minutes, and I'll give ye more."

"Where are we?" Gray light illumined a stone ceiling high above; slumped shapes at floor level were probably men, judging by the smell.

"A kirk."

"St. Stephen's," rumbled a voice from across the nave. "Inverness."

Iain had never been to Inverness but knew it was close to the bloody moor. How had he gotten here? Rustling and groans revealed the locations of more men. "Anyone here of Clan MacLeod of Raasay?" Iain clutched his head—the effort of speaking beyond a whisper renewed the pain. At least the rest of his body seemed intact. He coughed against the metallic smell of blood that surrounded him just as it had done on Culloden moor.

"I saw the laird of Clan MacLeod." A new voice, stronger than the last. "I was sure he was done for, too many up against him. Then one of his tacksmen raised sword and shield, his bonnie targe embossed in brass, shiny like gold, and plunged right into the mass of redcoats. The rest pulled the laird away, but the tacksman with the glittering shield disappeared."

His father. It was exactly what his father would have done as tacksman, staying close to his liege lord. And the targe was unmistakeable. He could picture the scene: the brass-studded targe, a gift from the laird, secure on his father's forearm, the family broadsword, bright in the sun, slicing at the enemy, driving them back.

For just a space of a few moments, until he was cut down.

"That was my father," Ian breathed.

"Sounds like a brave and braw man." The nearest man offered him another ladle of water.

"Aye, he was that." Ian drained the second offering. "Thank ye kindly."

At least his mother had gone on before. She would not have to bear this sorrow, though for him it was cold comfort, as he was orphaned now.

"Lad, if I dinna come back, will ye remember Robert Malcolm MacDonell of Glengarry's regiment?"

"Surely. And I am Ian MacLeod, son of William," he said in Gaelic, the language more real somehow to his heart. "But where might ye be going?"

"There is no food given us, only a few buckets of water. I am sorry, lad."

The words skirted his mind. Hunger was a constant, not to be fretted over.

Then Ian's innards chilled. MacDonell wasn't sorry for the lack of food. The English didn't care whether they lived or died. Which meant—

A low shudder preceded a sudden crack of light that quickly expanded and formed a doorway. Iain blinked at the startling brightness. Two figures appeared, one clearly armed.

"Robert MacDonell," a harsh voice barked.

MacDonell pushed himself to his knees. He gasped and hesitated. The shaft of light from the doorway fell on an ugly bayonet wound zigzagging down the side of his thigh. Blood coated the man's shin. Iain tucked an arm under MacDonell's armpit and lifted. Together they advanced toward the light.

"Pray for me." A mere whisper.

Pray? Reflexively, Iain grabbed at his chest; his rosary still hung from his neck, underneath his shirt. If only he could pray like his mother, who'd been taught prayers and Gaelic psalms by her Presbyterian parents. But would God hear, in any case?

Charles Stuart had said God was on their side. God appointed kings. God had appointed James and his son Charles. They couldn't lose. Seeing the prince's shining face that day last year in Edinburgh, Iain had felt a rush of certainty.

But clearly, Charles Stuart had been wrong.

Iain guessed what MacDonell was facing. Did his own doubts matter? As MacDonell drew even with the soldiers, Ian pulled the most familiar psalm from his mind and began to sing, the sound a croak to his ears: *"Is e Dia fhèin as buachaill dhomh, cha bhi mi ann an dìth..."*

As his voice strengthened, MacDonell limped outside. The door slammed shut, locking them all in darkness.

Iain continued singing the Twenty-Third Psalm, but his words weakened and finally died.

A shot rang out.

CHAPTER 2

VIRGINIA, MAY 1748

*M*ary Pickens squeezed her rag damp-dry and ran it along the edge of the windowpane. The ritual of cleaning calmed her, settled her. Sometimes it even made her forget.

"Mrs. Byrd, would you visit the house with me? The third story is finally complete." A too-familiar baritone issued from the hall.

Mary stilled the motion of her rag as the distant conversation between her master and mistress grew louder. They were approaching the open library door. Any nearer, and they'd see her inside.

The last thing she wanted was to appear to be eavesdropping. She was in enough trouble as it was.

"Mr. Byrd, if tomorrow suits you, then surely…"

They discussed which servants to take with them to the

new mansion, even larger than this one she labored to keep clean.

"I could not do without Celia, naturally." Mrs. Byrd's silky voice.

"And we'll take Chloe as well. I would pine away for her tarts otherwise."

Mary's heart ached. The cook was the closest thing to a friend in this place, now that her mistress's eyes had gone cold. She dipped her rag in the bucket, squeezed it gently, then resumed her cleaning as quietly as she could.

"What about Mary?" Eliza Byrd's tone was brittle as china.

Mary's indenture belonged to the Carters originally, purchased as a servant for Eliza Carter to bring into her marriage.

"Well, now..." He paused.

Her pulse thundered in her ears. Of course, her fate was his decision now.

"Would you mind greatly if I sold her contract?" His words smote Mary. What would happen to her now?

She straightened, trying to ease the ache in her back and legs. The rag slipped on the windowpane, squeaking, the sound seeming to carry throughout the house. Horrified, she continued cleaning.

"Oh, dearest, look how hard she works."

Mary focused on her task and tried to ignore the burning of her mistress's gaze.

"Do you recall Mr. Borden?" Mr. Byrd said. "His wife needs assistance just now."

Their voices grew fainter.

"The gentleman with the large property in the Shenandoah?"

Mary took a deep breath. Her master and mistress walked

away, and she heard no more. But she didn't need to. She'd heard enough to know that she'd be given to another man.

At least she'd get away from Mr. Byrd.

She dropped the rag in the bucket.

Once her new master saw her, he'd know.

* * *

THE MAN LOOMED in the hall, a stolid figure in a brown and muted green, simple pewter buttons marching over his belly. Next to him, Mr. Byrd shone like a goldfinch in his bright yellow waistcoat.

Hanging back in the shadows, Mary gripped her valise tightly. She had no other luggage. Her mother had taken the trunk when they'd been forced to split up at the dock after the Carters had purchased her contract from the captain. Someone else had purchased her mother's indenture, and a single letter had finally reached her. Her mother was working hard but was content with her situation.

"Write me with any further concerns." Mr. Byrd's voice had taken on a foreign cadence. He was three different people, with one tone of voice for his wife, one for men he sought to impress, and one … for her.

"Mary, meet Mr. Borden, your new employer."

Shoulders slightly hunched, she drew closer to the men in the hall. "Yes, sir. Pleased to meet you, sir." With her valise in hand, her curtsey was abbreviated. She straightened, and a wash of shame engulfed her as the shape of her body became plain under his gaze.

"She's a hearty worker." Mr. Byrd was suddenly fumbling, the polish of his voice wavering.

"To be sure." Mr. Borden's face and voice gave away nothing. "My driver is waiting." He reached for her valise.

Surprised, Mary released the bag into his care. Maybe he wasn't so bad. Or maybe—

She brushed that thought away and stumbled after him through the doorway. A scuffed and dusty carriage waited, harnessed to to a pair of sturdy black horses. They worried their bits as they stood in the traces. The coachman helped them in, and Mary scooted next to Mr. Borden inside the vehicle. She found a place for her feet amid the boxes and bundles and wondered how long their journey would be.

The morning shadows stretched before them along the narrow road. They were traveling west in a long tunnel of pine that opened up now and again to reveal the shimmering James River on the left.

She had so many questions. Where they were going. What Mr. Borden's plantation was like. But she didn't dare ask.

"We will stop the night in Richmond."

The night? How far would they be traveling?

Mr. Borden seemed to read the question on her face. "Mr. Byrd didn't tell you? My wife and I live in the Shenandoah Valley. Several days journey."

Shen— That name sounded familiar. Her mother's letter. Yes, it had come from there. "Is it large?"

"The valley? I suppose 'tis. Thirty miles wide, mayhap, but many miles long."

Her heart sank. Her mother could be anywhere.

But in the well of her shame, Mary saw a glimmer of hope. Mr. Borden was treating her as a person. Unlike Mr. Byrd, who only treated her kindly when—no, she would not think of that now. She forced her thoughts forward, wondering about the new place.

He continued, "Lots of folks in the valley come from

Ulster or thereabouts. Some, like you, served an indenture first."

Her her eyes pricked with moisture. Perhaps she'd find a home—eventually—in this valley.

But if she found her mother—she blinked away tears. How could she face her mother in this condition?

CHAPTER 3

isps of fog slid by outside the carriage window as the horses labored on the uphill slope. Mary tugged the lap blanket higher as her cloak was no longer sufficient for the chill of the mountains. Virginia winters were mild; at least they had been back on the Byrds' plantation.

Soon the fog cleared, and Mr. Borden announced a stop. "Rockfish Gap. We'll let the horses rest," he explained.

They clambered out, and Mary forgot the cold. To the west stretched a great vista: bluish ridges overlooking a vast expanse of patchwork—greens and yellows and browns.

"Are those fields?"

"Hmm? Oh, yes, some of them are fields. But some of what you see is grassland. It is said that the Indians used to set fires occasionally to keep the trees from taking over. Buffalo prefer grass."

Buffalo? She'd heard the word but couldn't imagine what they were.

"Buffalo rarely come into the valley nowadays." He

smiled, and the corners of his eyes crinkled. "We've a hide at the house."

Mr. Borden had become positively talkative compared to his long silences on the journey. And he didn't look at her, not in the way Mr. Byrd did. Maybe things would be better in this new place.

"Let's go. We'll be there at dusk, I reckon."

Dusk. Almost there. While she had begun to trust the mild-mannered Mr. Borden, she had no idea what his wife would be like. Mary slid her hand over her stomach. Her condition would be obvious immediately. Would the woman reject her? Would she be sent back to the Byrds?

Even if she weren't, what would happen when the baby came?

* * *

THE FIELDS WERE golden with the light of the setting sun, an orange ball dipping below the western ridges. The horses picked up their languid pace.

Split-rail fencing zigzagged along the sides of the track, enclosing frost-kissed fields of stubble. Behind a taller, sturdier fence, a beautiful black horse cantered, its tail raised like a flag. One of the carriage horses nickered a greeting.

Structures appeared. A red house dominated the property; other plainer buildings surrounded it. One was clearly a barn. The home was in no wise as large or prestigious as the Byrds'. In fact, it looked like a simple dwelling, enlarged by a connecting room with an open passageway in between. Sweet memories of Ireland—before the disaster—brushed Mary's mind.

"The Red House," Mr. Borden announced cheerfully.

"Built by my wife's first husband. Painted with clay from the property."

"Do you grow tobacco?"

"Not here. I have property elsewhere. This was originally my wife's, and we grow hemp as well as foodstuffs. You'll meet her soon, as well as my stepchildren."

Stepchildren? But her musings were interrupted by an explosion of activity around the buildings. A swarm of people—well, no, just several women and a man, plus several children—converged on the still-moving carriage.

The sight of a lad of perhaps twelve summers, light brown hair tousled by the breeze, caused her heart to jump in her chest. As he approached, she studied him. No, he looked nothing at all like her dead brother, not really. "Mr. Borden! Ma says I am to help you."

A broad smile rolled back the years from the man's face. Perhaps he wasn't that old after all. "Surely you may." He stepped out of the carriage and helped Mary down. "And greet Miss Mary, if you will."

The lad scrutinized her. "Will she help Ma?"

"Your manners," his stepfather prompted.

"Sammy—Samuel McDowell, at your service." He bobbed his head in greeting. "Welcome to the Red House, Miss ..."

"Miss Mary," Mr. Borden prompted.

Introduction complete, Mr. Borden handed Samuel a heavy-looking sack. The lad headed for the house, seemingly unencumbered by the parcel over his shoulder.

Then the coachman and another servant took over the unloading. Mr. Borden grabbed Mary's valise and directed her by the elbow toward the house. The warm smell of burning oak and hickory mixed with savory odors awakened her belly. She was always hungry now.

"There is someone you will be glad to see."

What did he mean by that? His wife?

There was indeed a woman approaching, a large woman —no, a woman swollen with child. Her smile beautified a face already attractive; a fine lace cap did little to conceal blond locks. A stained apron belled out over her wool skirt. Clearly, this woman was not like Eliza Byrd, who disdained labor.

"Welcome home, Mr. Borden," she said, her voice musical with Ireland.

Homesickness tinged with the unfamiliar feeling of hope swept over Mary. She blinked rapidly.

"This is Mary Pickens."

Mary's breath caught in her throat as she waited for Mrs. Borden to notice her condition. Then the woman smiled, and grabbing her hands, drew her close.

"So you're Mary." Her gray-green eyes were kind and steady. "I'm that glad you're here."

Hadn't she noticed?

Mrs. Borden turned and gestured toward another woman.

A familiar face.

Mary stepped forward. "Ma!" Could her mother really be here? Her throat constricted.

Ma smiled broadly, crow's feet framing her warm brown eyes. Her nut-brown hair, so like her own, was touched by threads of gray Mary had never noticed before.

"Ma? I did not know you—"

Mrs. Borden slipped away.

"Mr. Borden purchased my contract that day on the docks. He helped me track you down."

Her mother's gaze took in her form, and Mary could tell the moment her mother realized her condition. Her expression sagged. She smiled, but the smile was sad.

"I was afraid for you—"

"The Carters were good to me."

"Mr. Borden was concerned when we discovered Miss Carter had married and your contract now belonged to Mr. Byrd."

The contract. Mary had always been glad not to be in perpetual slavery, like Chloe, but the contract could be extended for running away—or rebellion. The bondage was real.

Her mother gazed off into the distance. "I worried for your virtue."

Guilt welled up as Mr. Byrd's face flashed into her mind. She'd told herself it wasn't her fault, but the reality was, she hadn't resisted Mr. Byrd's advances. Not truly. She could have struggled more. She could have screamed. But her fear froze her in place.

"You'll be safe here," her mother soothed. "The Bordens are good people. 'Tis almost like home."

Mary nodded. Safe. She'd be safe. But things would never be the same again.

CHAPTER 4

THE *GILDART*, NORTH ATLANTIC, JULY 1747

*S*alt spray dashed against Iain MacLeod's face as he gripped the rail. His nausea receded while out on deck, though those moments in the sun and the breeze were limited, and only two men were allowed up at a time. The fierce sun of summer beat down on his uncovered head, but he didn't mind. Below decks the stench of unwashed bodies plus the fetid odor of the hold wafting through the crevices of the ship made the escape to the deck a blissful privilege.

The *Gildart* was a slaver, and there were a hundred poor souls in the hold, in addition to the Scottish indentures crowded aft of the crew's hammocks. Jacobites all, they were prisoners, and prisoners were not treated with any thought to their comfort. But unlike the Africans, only a few wore shackles, and the strongest among them were pressed into the lowliest of tasks. Iain had already scrubbed the forward heads twice, a nasty job, but at least he'd been out in the air.

And they were fed more if they worked. Some, half-starved from prison, had actually regained health and strength on ship's biscuit, salt pork, and Sunday pease porridge. But a few were very weak, even dying.

Most of his fellow shipmates were from Arbroath prison, where he had been taken after being tossed into a kirk in Inverness. Some he recognized, but only one he knew well, Andrew Brown, a middle-aged farmer who'd been picked up on "suspicion."

Brown was on deck now, near the bow, the brisk air threatening to tease the fine brown hair from his tail. He'd found a bit of string to keep his hair tied back; his clothing was tattered but as neat as he could make it. Like Brown, most of the prisoners fought for some scrap of cleanliness and normalcy. A contraband needle was passed around, necessary for repairs to clothing. One of their number, a university student who'd joined in the fighting, recited to them from Shakespeare, Homer, or the Bible in the darkness below. It kept them sane.

Brown took a few steps toward him, still looking out to sea. "Notice anything different about the water?"

Iain checked his peripheral vision. Their minder, a crewman with a club, was standing lazily near the mizzen-mast, not close enough to hear. Then Ian looked at the ocean. Something was different, but he couldn't put his finger on it.

"Look at the shadows."

The shadow of the mainmast lay amidships and to starboard. *Wait.* Afternoon shadows normally pointed *behind* them.

Brown raised a brow. "See? We're headed north. And the color of the water is different, forbye."

Yes! The water had lost its rich blue color and now resembled the greenish blue of the channel off the Isle of Raasay. A favorite spot on the edge of his father's property came to mind, a cliff overlooking a narrow beach, lively gray waves dashing up and back playfully. And just across the way, the Isle of Skye.

He blinked, and the image was gone, but the color remained. He turned west—but saw nothing on the horizon.

"Ye canna see it," Brown said, following his gaze. "But it's there."

He strained his eyes—was there a smudge above the blue? He knew they were headed to Maryland, but what would happen to them there? He'd be at the mercy of whoever purchased his contract. At least he was alive, unlike most of the poor souls led out one by one to meet their fate in Inverness. Iain and another man had been sent to prison, and from thence sentenced to seven years of labor in the colonies. They'd shared a kind of brotherhood while in prison and on the ship, helping one another and rehashing the war. Ian had learned more about the conflict while in prison than he had when he'd been a participant.

"If only more of the Campbells had joined the Cause," he muttered reflexively. Most were traitors against their own people and against their true king, King James. Not that it mattered now, but it still rankled. The Duke of Argyll, laird of the Campbells, had supported the German usurpers from the beginning, even before Sheriffmuir.

"Aye, or the French," Brown said mildly, cutting a glance at the guard. Their time was almost up. "But all that's behind us now. We've a chance—"

"After seven years of slavery—"

"Even so. Ye'll not have to hide that wee bit of plaid here, I'm thinking."

Iain became conscious of his belt, where a piece of MacLeod tartan lay hidden. He'd carefully slit the leather and crafted a hiding place. The Duke of Cumberland hadn't been satisfied by the butchery at Culloden. He'd rampaged the hills, searching for supporters, jailing bystanders like Brown, and burning crofts. When Parliament had banned the wearing of the traditional Scottish tartan, it felt as if the Sassenachs were trying to stamp them out as a people.

And largely, except for traitors like the Campbells, they'd succeeded.

A tiny ember of hope flared as he thought on Brown's words. He could be a Scot in this new land—

Except.

Iain laid his hand on his chest, feeling the hard rowan wood beads that made up the rosary hidden under his shirt.

Brown's eyes followed his motion. "Aye, laddie, this wide new land will be better for Scots, but I'm thinking, dinna tell them ye're a Papist. Not even in Maryland."

Ian's shoulders sagged. Brown was Church of England, but most of the Jacobites on board ship were Catholic.

He stared at the waves, the wind whipping the tops into gray foam. God was against them. God was against *him.* In prison he'd learned that Raasay had been attacked by Cumberland. Livestock taken, the manor and the houses burned.

His beautiful home was gone.

He ripped the rosary from his neck and threw it into the sea.

CHAPTER 5

ANNE ARUNDEL COUNTY, MARYLAND, 1748

The marshy, salty east wind carried memories of home as Iain thrust his hoe into the sandy loam at the base of the corn. The familiar smell of the sea caused the Maryland plantation to fade, and he was once again on the broad, rolling moor of the isle of Raasay, seeking out a lost ewe.

He loved the stubborn wooly creatures, and he knew the way of horses especially. The way they thought and felt, the things that startled them, the things that intrigued them. But for the past year at Belle Voir, his toil had been with the earth. He was slowly grasping the way of the soil, too, but it was a harsh mistress, because it was not his choice.

It was not his home.

His only consolation was the presence of the man in the field with him. Andrew Brown's contract had been purchased along with his. Granted, the man was Church of

England, and did not speak Gaelic, but he understood much of it, and he knew the ache of missing his homeland.

Iain wiped his forehead. The winter had been short but sharp, and now summer's air settled like a cloying blanket on his shoulders. Nearby, Brown's motions slowed. He was an older man and couldn't bear the work as well as Iain, who had managed to put on both inches and pounds over the months they'd been here.

At least they were decently fed, a mercy he appreciated after the lean time of the war and the privations of prison.

Thrack! Thrack!

Brown paused and straightened, turning toward the sound, which came from the outbuildings near their cabin.

Thrack... thrack!

A curl of dread rolled down Ian's neck as he visualized the only thing that could make that sound: the overseer's long whip. He saw it every day, hanging on a peg at the cabin doorway. The overseer shared a large, plain cabin with the white laborers—himself and Brown—and the whip was always ready to hand.

And never used—until now.

Would the overseer ever use it on *them?*

Iain chopped at a stubborn weed, willing the disturbing sound to fade, hoping he'd be spared the sound of screaming.

The field faded, and he was back on Culloden moor, navigating between piles of dead bodies supervised by flies and crows, trying to keep hidden from the roving bands of redcoats who sought to extinguish any last ember of life.

Occasional screams or gunshots tore through the air, but mostly the dying was done quietly.

Iain squeezed the hard wood of the hoe in his hands until the horrible lashing stopped.

Who had been punished? A dozen or so slaves lived in the

barracks-like cabin a bowshot from their own. Which of them had done something serious enough to warrant it?

Brown caught his gaze and shrugged. An understanding passed between them—they wouldn't fuss or act as if they noticed. Brown turned his attention back to his labor, and Iain did likewise.

* * *

IAIN POURED a dipperful of water over his head at the well before picking up the buckets and carrying them to the cabin, his muscles aching from fatigue. As he entered, Brown paused, then pulled off his shirt and hung it on a peg to dry. Ian put down the buckets and found his own dry shirt— aired, but not clean—and changed. They might be given a half day off on Saturday, since it was neither plowing nor harvest. Ian looked forward to taking his filthy clothes to the stream.

He joined Brown at the kitchen table, and wordlessly they prepared a simple meal, chopping vegetables to add to pease porridge. He hoped the overseer, Arkin, would bring some pork or fish—they had no meat in the cabin.

But thinking of the overseer made his innards cramp. He cut a glance to the doorway. The horsewhip was still missing.

He was making chicory coffee when a muffled creak and thud made him turn.

It was Arkin, and his face was unreadable. His whip tucked under one arm, he carried a basket. "Chicken."

He placed the basket on the table, then reached for one of the water buckets. "I'll refill this later."

There was blood on the whip in his hand. He plunged his hands and the handle of the whip into the bucket, then cleansed the length of the leather, inch by inch.

No one spoke as Brown ladled out the porridge and set the bowls on the table.

Arkin hung the whip back on its peg and sat down. They ate in silence, the only sound the dripping of the wet whip.

"It was Aaron."

"Wha—" Iain shut his mouth abruptly. Most days he could forget the difference in their station—an indentured servant was like a slave in some ways, but his servitude was limited. Since coming to the colonies, Ian had discovered another thing, too. His skin color made a difference. There was an advantage to being white.

But Arkin was a free man, a hired man, and spent a fair amount of time in the Big House. Iain studied him. He wasn't truly their ally—he represented the master. While he was never cruel, he was sharp-eyed and efficient.

Across the table, Brown's eyes were wide. "Aaron the coachman?"

"What, you thought it'd be Samson or Matthew?"

Arkin had just named two of the field hands who worked in the tobacco fields.

"Aaron has a wife, one of Duvall's people. He was given a pass to visit her. Never came back." He snorted. "The blockhead. He wears fine livery, eats as well as I do, enjoys the pleasures of a wife, and decides it's not enough."

The overseer rose and poured himself some coffee. "Mr. Ross is one of the best masters in all of Anne Arundel County. Why should he run?"

"Where is he now?"

"Aaron?" Arkin sneered over his cup. "Being doctored by Miss Anna, the master's own daughter. He has it good here. I'll never understand it."

While the whip continued to drip, Iain stared into his empty bowl.

He understood.

Slavery was slavery.

* * *

THE YEAR WAS SETTLING into autumn and the corn harvest was almost completed when Iain was summoned into Mr. Ross's study. He'd only been into the Big House twice—once, when he first arrived, and again to retrieve a salve from the cook. Every few months the housekeeper came to the cabin, bringing supplies—foodstuffs, blankets, and odds and ends that made life possible, if not easy. So he knew the grim face that greeted him at the back door.

Iain followed the housekeeper down the hall to an open doorway. What was this about? Was he in trouble? For a moment he was able to study Mr. Ross's face as he sat scrutinizing an open ledger.

The man was not old, but creases dug into his face, and silver glinted at his temples. The slaves whispered that he'd not recovered from the death of his wife two years before. His daughters, both of marriageable age, had recovered their smiles as they exercised their horses and puttered in the gardens, but not he.

Ross looked up, his cravat crooked. "Oh. Yes, come in." His brows rose. "You've grown." He waved vaguely to a chair. "Do sit."

Iain sat carefully on the fine chair in front of the desk, hoping its spindly legs would sustain his weight.

Ross pulled out a large piece of parchment and searched it. "How old are you?"

"I'll be eighteen next month, sir."

"And over five years left on this contract."

Iain's heart jumped into his throat.

"I know you have been a faithful man..." Ross frowned, not looking him in the eye. "I have arranged to sell your contract."

What? Iain's throat dried. As much as he resented servitude, this *was* a good place. His heart raced and his palms became moist as he waited for the man across from him to continue.

"I had to, you see, and one of the hands, as well."

"Where... who?" Ian wiped his hands on his breeches.

"A relation in South Carolina needs a laborer." Ross finally met his gaze. "I've a parting gift."

He opened a drawer and pulled out a book bound in green leather and a small drawstring bag. He pushed both across the desk to Iain.

"A New Testament. And Jesuit bark, for the fever."

Iain's belly curdled. *For the fever?* He took both items, feeling disembodied as if he were dreaming.

"You leave next week."

CHAPTER 6

THE SHENANDOAH VALLEY

*M*ary Pickens shifted on the hard pew, the words of the minister beating upon her shoulders.

"Can you be wise and yet not consider your eternal end? Nay, can you pretend to so much as common sense while you sell your eternal salvation for the sordid pleasures of a few flying years?"

Sordid pleasures. Pleasures with Mr. Byrd? No, it hadn't been her idea, but—

"Awake, you sluggish, careless souls! The house over your head is in a flame! The hand of God is lifted up in wrath against you!"

She cut a glance to either side. Everyone sat transfixed as if drinking in the man's message. Perhaps they were all righteous, all clean, without any fear of wrath.

"If you love yourselves, prevent the stroke! Vengeance is

at your backs… return to God! Make Christ and mercy your friends in time, if you love your lives!"

Finally the minister concluded his message, and Mary took a deep breath. Her belly grumbled. She'd never heard such long sermons. Was it sinful to get hungry and restless listening to preaching?

Probably.

There was nothing in her that was any good at all.

The service over, Mary followed the Bordens out into the autumn sunshine. Surrounded by her children, Magdalena Borden glowed, a swan with her cygnets. She laughed and visited with the other women as they cooed over her new baby. Mrs. Borden had given birth only a month ago but was back at church.

Finally, the family scrambled into the vehicles, a carriage for the young ones, a wagon for the servants. Ma minded the young infant, Elizabeth, in the back of the wagon, and to Mary's surprise, Mrs. Borden clambered onto the wagon seat instead of choosing the carriage. Then she remembered Mrs. Borden's remarks the previous day about looking forward to riding her beloved stallion once again. The woman was a godly matriarch but a little eccentric, too.

"Aw, Ma," Samuel complained. He enjoyed driving.

"Shush," Mrs. Borden warned. "I need the air. You may ride Galahad back."

This occasioned a smile on Samuel's face, but a frown creased James's. The younger lad rode the gentle gelding whenever he could.

"No' a cross word do I wish to hear, especially on the Sabbath."

Soon the family was sorted, the younger children scrambling into the carriage with their father. Mary joined her mother in the wagon bed.

The sight of Mrs. Borden's new babe in her mother's arms brought a flush to Mary's face. The borrowed clothing she wore swallowed up her slim form, disguising her own growing bulge. For her a baby was not a joy.

The oversized clothing was Mrs. Borden's idea. "I dinna like deceit," she'd said. "But I want you to hear the Word preached, and for now, 'twill be easy enough to hide your situation." She harrumphed. "'Twas not your fault, I'm sure!"

How the woman presumed to know her innocence was a mystery, but Mary'd overheard the Bordens discussing Mr. Byrd once.

"Just like his father, I'm sure..." Mr. Borden had said.

His wife clucked in agreement. They didn't approve of the man.

Mrs. Borden slapped the reins against the horses' rumps and they were off. They traveled in silence for several miles, and Mary lifted her face to enjoy the warmth of the sun. A last memory of summer spilled over the rolling countryside, banishing the autumn chill, and the guilt plaguing her ebbed away.

The infant in Ma's arms wriggled and cooed. Mary had been mesmerized by the child ever since little Elizabeth had made her appearance, a tiny red stranger who had turned the household upside down. Even the chores were redistributed, with Mary taking over Ma's heavier tasks.

Elizabeth opened her eyes, looked at Mary, and smiled.

This stranger was a... *person.*

The stranger in her own belly kicked.

Oh. The wonder of new life expanded to include her own bulging middle.

Hello, little one.

* * *

WEEKS SPED BY, and the weather cooled. But the work remained.

"Take mine." Mrs. Borden's hands were buried in the wool of her knitting, but her chin jerked toward her green-and-blue tartan cloak hung near the door. "Yours is too thin."

Thin was a kind description for the brown cast-off cloak Mary owned. Threadbare and ragged at the hems, it served well enough for mild weather, but a frigid December wind was blowing.

"Thank you." Mary eased the beautiful garment off its peg gently. It was large, but if she stood straight, the hem would not reach the ground.

For the past month, she'd only had to care for the chickens and fetch water and wood; her duties were now focused on the mistress, the babe, and the other children. Her mother cooked, cleaned, and did the laundry, and a new hire milked the cows.

Carefully Mary closed the door behind her. Mrs. Borden said the cloak was the Campbell tartan, the colors a badge of the clan. Presumably the woman was a Campbell then. She hadn't explained her family history.

Mary headed toward the woodpile, the brisk air full of the smell of cut wood.

Thunk.

The new hire, the "McKee lad," as Mrs. Borden referred to him, was splitting logs, the axe flashing in the cold sunlight. His dark head bent over his work, strong shoulders flexing under the stained leather of his jacket.

Thunk.

Lad? No, he was a well-formed man.

She hesitated, and at that moment he looked up, hazel eyes warm. He gave her a friendly grin.

"G'morning."

She found her voice. "G'morning. I-I came for wood."

He thrust the blade of the axe into the stump and headed for the stack of seasoned wood. "How much?"

"The box is almost empty."

He filled his arms and she trailed after him with a few more sticks.

"Thank you."

He slowed as he neared the door. "I'm Simon McKee." His gaze searched her face.

"Miss Pickens. Mary Pickens."

"I'll leave this here." He placed the wood on the step.

As he returned to his work, she studied his broad shoulders and the roll of his gait.

A cool breeze struck her cheek, but her heart was warm. A new and puzzling feeling.

* * *

A WEEK LATER, Mr. Borden returned from Williamsburg. "The snow started just as I reached Rockfish Gap." He hung his greatcoat on a peg and warmed his hands at the fire. "I made it back just in time."

Mary set the kettle on the hook over the fire for tea. The wind picked at the eaves and slid around the corners of the house, whistling and grumbling. She hoped Simon was warm. The hired men slept in a small cabin on the property while Mary and her mother had snug pallets in the house.

Mrs. Borden greeted her husband. "Say hello to Miss Eliza."

He lifted the babe. "Hello, Miss Elizabeth, fair one, breaker of hearts. Why, you've grown."

He'd been gone only two weeks.

"Papa! Papa!" James dashed into the room and jerked to a

halt. He made a clumsy obeisance, a ten-year-old version of adult manners. "Welcome home."

Sarah entered with the dignity of a child on the cusp of womanhood and bobbed a tiny curtsey.

Their stepfather—the only father they remembered—bowed slightly, pewter waistcoat buttons winking in the firelight.

He set Elizabeth down and scooped up Martha, who was six and trailed a blanket.

"Papa, I'm nae babe."

Mary's mouth twitched into a faint smile. The stolid Mr. Borden thawed around his children. She found a rag and wiped the floor where his greatcoat had dripped, then made the tea.

Mr. Borden sipped his tea. "I need to see to things," he said once his cup was drained.

Things was his word for the farm: the hired men, the animals, the fences. He rarely labored with his hands, but his eye searched out every need. He would not rest until he knew all was settled and secure.

"Sammy went to see to the horses." Mrs. Borden adjusted her clothing to feed the baby.

He nodded and left.

"Come, Mary. Pour yourself a cup of tea and sit."

Mary obeyed, fearing she was in trouble. But no. She'd had to remind herself again and again that her new mistress was not that sort. The warm mug felt good in her hands, and slowly her tight muscles relaxed.

"I've a tale to tell." Mrs. Borden lifted the babe to her shoulder and patted its back. "About my mother."

Little Eliza belched. Mrs. Borden smiled, and she placed the infant in the wooden cradle at her feet.

"The cloak. The Campbell tartan," she began. "Lovely,

isn't it? Green and blue, the beauty of earth and sky, the beauty of Scotland—and the valley."

Mary waited. Magdalena Borden was a friendly, voluble woman, and would not stay silent long.

"My mother was a Campbell. Daughter of an important man, but not the duke. Lady Campbell, they called her, before she married my father for love." She picked up her cup. "Any more tea?"

Mary poured the last of the clear brown liquid.

"She gave me this cloak. Told me to remember my heritage." She took a cautious sip. "And she told me to remember something else." Her gaze went to the cloak on its peg. "Jesus gave us a cloak. His cloak—His robe of righteousness."

How could Jesus give someone a cloak?

"Not a physical garment." Mrs. Borden seemed to read the question on her face. "A spiritual one. Ye've heard the preaching. Ye ken God's wrath on sinners. How are we to escape?"

"The cross?" Mary knew it was the right answer, though her heart still quailed, feeling the weight of her sins.

"Aye. But even before Christ died in our place, He lived a perfect, sinless life. He lived in our place as well. This righteousness is the robe Christ gives to us. Like a cloak it covers us, covers all our sin and shame. God looks down and sees only the righteousness of His Son."

Mary looked at the cloak. *A covering.*

This was good news.

If only she could truly believe it.

* * *

JANUARY HAD ALMOST CLOSED its doors with a smile when the weather shifted. Mary grabbed two empty buckets and went outside only to be confronted by strange clouds to the north.

It was warm; one neighbor had started plowing. But it was a false spring, and on the Bordens' property, the hired men continued with the winter chores, mending fences and tack, caring for the animals, and sharpening plowshares.

Mary headed for the spring. The well water was sweet but needed to be hauled out of the depths. She could do it, but her huge midsection made everything difficult. Sometimes Simon helped her, always with a ready smile, but today she didn't see him around.

The path seemed longer today, the walk tiring.

At the spring she crouched, her belly jutting forward awkwardly. She dipped the buckets into the ice-cold water, wondering how long it would be until the baby was born. Ma had whispered, *Soon.*

Will the babe look like Mr. Byrd? The horrible thought could no longer be pushed away.

Frigid tendrils of air puffed against her cheeks as she struggled to stand. Above, bare branches sighed and creaked in the wind.

As she plodded back to the house, she forced herself to think about Mr. Byrd. His hair was dark, as dark as her mother's. Her own was a bit lighter, reflecting her father's, whose curly locks she remembered to be lighter still, almost blond.

Her stomach seized up, and she paused. A wave of nausea passed through her, and she lowered the buckets. She leaned against a beech tree until she felt steady again.

The entire northern sky was a heaving mass of white, gray, and a strange ochre color. The wind swirled and eddied around her, teasing the hem of her cloak, and sending needles of sharp cold into her clothing.

Fear gripped her. She needed to get back inside. She grabbed the handles of the water buckets and wrestled them up. They were strangely heavy, but she managed to get up the path and into the open.

As snowflakes swirled around her, sudden pressure gripped her around the middle, and she staggered. She set the buckets down and took a slow breath.

Was this it? Was the baby coming?

She'd make it to the house, she had to. Step by step.

She picked up the buckets, took three more steps.

Pressure slammed her. Like a giant hand, the grip tightened over her belly, intensifying into pain.

One of the buckets slipped from her grasp and sloshed its contents over the dead grass at her feet.

Mary gulped the air. She needed to focus. Barren limbs of trees stretched up around her, and she could not see the red of the house. But it could not be far. She waited until the pain eased and picked up the fallen bucket. No time to fuss over it or return for more water.

Icy pellets stung her face, and the gusts fought to get past her cloak.

She'd just glimpsed the house through the trees when another wave hit. This time, she dropped both the buckets and fell to her knees, groaning.

A sudden blast of icy wind blew the clasp of the heavy cloak undone, and the Campbell plaid danced like wings at her sides. Mary gasped, her belly on fire and the rest of her plunged in ice.

"Miss Mary!" A presence.

Simon's worried face appeared before her. His gaze scanned her form.

"'Tis my time."

His frown resolved into comprehension.

With his help, she was walking again, crunching fresh footprints into the fresh snow. But her heart ached with loss. Whether Simon knew of her state before, he certainly knew it now.

He would never smile at her again.

* * *

"She's with Mrs. Wilkins." Mr. Borden's voice came from the other room. The front door clattered shut.

A tendril of frigid air curled into the room where Mary lay on her pallet, sweating in her shift.

"The only other midwife is Maggie McClure." Mrs. Borden's voice sounded strained.

"There's a foot of snow already, not to mention the wind. Twenty miles—"

"Aye, I ken it. Maggie's too far away. I know what to do."

"I'll get more wood."

Wood and water were her responsibility. But the next pain drove all thought out of Mary's mind.

"Hold my hands," Ma murmured. "Breathe. We'll take care of you."

They moved her to the birthing chair, and her sense of time vanished. Only pain remained. Mary was vaguely aware of her mother and Mrs. Borden bustling about.

"Mama… Mama." It was too much. It would never end.

"Almost there." Mrs. Borden's voice.

Her mother held her shoulders from behind. "The babe's coming."

"Push, now, lassie."

Mary groaned and obeyed.

38

"Again."

Mary squeezed the arms of the birthing chair. Each push seemed feeble, but she felt a glimmer of hope.

Almost there, almost there.

A tremendous wave of pressure came and went.

"A boy," Mrs. Borden said. "A wee laddie."

Mary's heart leapt. Why wasn't it crying? She yearned to hold the child.

"Wake up, little mannie."

A thin cry filled the room.

"What's his name?" Her mother's voice.

"Thomas." Her voice sounded like a croak in her ears. "Thomas is his name."

Her father's name.

Then he was in her arms, and an unspeakable warmth flooded her. She loved him, a powerful, unexpected feeling.

She looked up at her mother, whose eyes reflected concern.

Mary understood. Ice-cold reality shattered her joy. She was unwed—Thomas was illegitimate.

CHAPTER 7

BELMONT PLANTATION, SOUTH CAROLINA

A flash of white wings marked the rise of a heron behind the cypress and birch trees sheltering the Cooper River.

Free. The birds were free. But Iain MacLeod had four years left on his contract. Four long years.

And Henry Jackson was sick.

Iain walked to the indigo field in the gray dawn light. He'd left Henry sweating on his pallet, the older man deep in fevered dreams.

Iain had no more Jesuit bark to give him.

He reached the rows of purple-topped shrubs. The small hopeful flowers had appeared just last week, and Miss Eliza —more properly, Mrs. Pinckney—had smiled at the sight.

One row over, Hector trimmed the plants, his dark back exposed to the air. Joe worked nearby, wearing a shirt as he always did. What Joe never explained—but everyone knew—

41

was that he'd been whipped as a young man and did not want the scars exposed.

They were both fiercely loyal to Mrs. Pinckney.

All said she'd been the first to plant indigo in the country at her father's plantation, figuring out what it needed here in the low country between the rivers. Last year Henry and Iain had learned the trick of the dye, soaking the leaves until the vaguely sweet-sour stench of fermentation scented the air above the barrels. Then came the filtering, adding lime, decanting, drying.

The brilliant blue powder they produced surprised Iain, the alchemy a strange but delightful magic. Who would have imagined that a green plant could yield such a thing?

But today any joy in his work was gone. Henry's recurring fevers underscored the fact of their bondage. The Jesuit bark had eased each attack, but now it was gone, and he was totally dependent on the goodness of master and mistress.

Iain had made the decision last night.

"I'm going to ask Mrs. Pinckney for Jesuit bark."

Henry wrapped his blanket tight, despite the July heat. "I dreamed of my sister just now." His dead sister.

"Rosey says stinking gum doesna do much good for the country fever." Sometimes Ian spotted the African slaves with a bag of the noxious herb about their necks. "But we know the bark works."

"'Precious in the sight of the Lord is the death of his saints.'"

Now Henry was quoting Scripture again.

Sometimes Iain read to the man from the small green book. Henry could write his name but struggled over the tiny words. Ian's eyes and reading skills were better, but he had no notion what propitiation meant. Or impute.

Even as David also describeth the blessedness of the man, unto whom God imputeth righteousness without works.

Without works? Righteousness without works?

So he'd asked Henry about it, who smiled. "By grace. All of grace."

Iain turned this over in his mind as he went to the tool shed for a scythe and some twine. It was time to cut and bundle the indigo. He returned and began trimming back the plants carefully. Ideally, the plant would regrow, and they'd harvest more just before the first frost.

It was easy work compared to rice or tobacco. Even so, by noon his shoulders and back ached. He tied up the bundles and brought them to the indigo shed, looking forward to a long draught of switchel or watered ale. Every morning the cook prepared jugs for the hands.

He found Mrs. Pinckney instead. She was puttering in the shed, checking supplies. A married woman with a babe in arms, she still found time to supervise the indigo and the mulberry orchard, necessary for her newest project, producing silk.

"Mac."

"Aye, ma'am."

"We've plenty lime, but we'll need more for the autumn cutting."

She wasn't truly speaking to him, just thinking through the list of supplies she needed.

He glanced at the shelves. "Perhaps cheesecloth."

More peering and puttering. "Yes, I believe so. More cheesecloth."

Then she looked at him, really looked. "Where's Mr. Jackson?"

"Feeling poorly." No, not poorly—the man would die

without the bark. "He's got the country fever bad. He... he may not make it."

Her eyes widened. "The ague? I'll fetch hickory ashes."

"Missus, I-I had good results with Jesuit's bark. But I have no more."

Her expression changed. "I've heard of it. With a name like that, folks consider it papist. I can't be asking for that in Charles Town." She picked up a coil of twine and studied it.

Papist. He should have known.

She looked up. "Does it have another name?"

Hope flashed through him. The woman knew plants and all their names. "Aye. Peruvian bark."

"Well, then. I'll go tomorrow."

Iain returned to his work. Staring at the indigo, he forced a prayer.

Help, Lord. Help Henry. But why should God listen to him?

* * *

HENRY JACKSON DIED in the night. Iain rose to see him cold and still, a peaceful expression on his face.

Iain felt hollow inside. For the first time, he realized how he'd appreciated the older man. His patience, his kind witticisms, his faith. He rarely complained, and when he did it was couched in humor.

Anger surged within him. Like Belle Voir, Belmont Plantation was a good place compared to most. But the bondage —and its effects—chafed.

Of course, he wouldn't be here at all if it weren't for the dirty redcoats on Culloden Moor. The Duke of Cumberland and his minions, rampaging over Scotland.

The country fever—the malaria—took both rich and poor. He knew that. But disease seemed to prey on servants more than others, especially white indentures. Would he survive his contract?

Only God knew. He fingered the green Testament. Sometimes he wished to rip out the pages, burn the book. Other times, he ached for the elusive hope it spoke of.

He pulled on his stained breeches and ran his fingers through his hair. He needed to tell Mrs. Pinckney about Henry.

He headed toward the house. The two-story red brick home with painted shutters boasted flowers and a crushed oyster shell walk in the front. He circled to the kitchen door, the servants' entrance.

The smell of bacon greeted him.

"Rosey ... Mr. Jackson is dead."

The dark-skinned cook whirled. "What?"

"Mistress needs to know."

Rosey wiped her hands on her apron. She gave her attention to the bacon, lifting the pan off the fire. "Dead? You sure? Of course you're sure... A shroud, he needs a shroud. Betsy can—" Her eyes filled with tears. "Sweet man, such a sweet man. I'll get the missus."

Iain stared stupidly at the fire and the abandoned bacon, the kitchen suddenly empty and still. But he didn't have to wait long.

"Mr. Iain, sir, she's gone! She done gone to Charles Town at the crack o' dawn!"

Mr. Pinckney was already in town, where he spent much of his time. What were they to do now? "Is Mr. Williams here?"

"Quash? Yessir, he here. I 'spect he'll be up soon to eat." She placed the bacon back on the fire.

Quash was the most trusted of the slaves. He'd been given

his freedom and baptized with the name of John Williams. But the hands still called him Quash.

"Who's asking 'bout me?" Quash was tall and very dark, still in the prime of his youth. He wore a butternut waistcoat over his shirt; his breeches were patched but clean.

"Mr. Jackson is dead," Ian said.

"The ague?"

"Aye."

Rosey poked at the sizzling bacon with more force than was necessary. "What do we do? They might be gone days, and him going to stink!"

"We bury him." Quash sighed heavily. "I'll get the fellows to dig."

Rosey scooped the bacon out of the pan vigorously and cracked eggs into the grease left behind. "Don't got no minister. He woulda liked words spoken over him." She whisked the eggs. "Quash, can you do it? Speak the words?"

Quash looked at Iain. "You has a Testament. You speak the words."

Iain's stomach tightened. The other man could read. But for some reason, he'd chosen Iain, and there was no gainsaying him.

In any case, Iain had no heart to argue.

* * *

IAIN SAT on his pallet with the green Testament in his lap. He had no idea what to say. Through the window, he glimpsed the men digging in the tiny graveyard adjacent to the family's burial plot. The place slaves were laid to rest.

He was supposed to "speak the words." What words would help? The man was dead.

With a sudden clarity, Iain knew Henry was with his

Maker. With his Redeemer. At peace. His own heart knew no peace, but Henry had certainly lived with an eye fixed on heaven.

He should honor that. But how?

Ian stood and paced the small cabin. He stopped at the window and ran his fingers through his hair.

Unbidden, his mind went back to the salty windswept moors of Raasay, the heather-studded rolling pastures, home to hundreds of sheep. Shaggy hieland cows grazed the choicest spots, their milk feeding the bairns and pressed into rich cheese. But the sheep were the wealth of the island; their wool clothed everyone and was sold to weavers as far away as Edinburgh.

The sheep.

Is e Dia fhèin as buachaill dhomh ...

The Twenty-Third Psalm.

He put down the book and grabbed his comb. He had no fine clothing, but he'd comb and queue his hair as best he could. He owned a frayed waistcoat he wore to church; he'd wear it today.

In a quarter hour he was as clean and presentable as he could make himself. He found the psalms in the tiny Testament, tucked away at the end. Then he left, heart thudding.

The small graveyard was thronged. Rosey had changed her kerchief and apron; Betsy wore a cheerful yellow print dress; the hands, Joe and Hector, wore the only clothes they had, their respect revealed by their posture.

Quash seemed taller than he was, standing at the head of the open grave. Beside it, the body lay shrouded in coarse linsey. There had been no time to make a coffin.

Iain took a place at the foot.

He swallowed and found his place. "The Lord is my shepherd..."

The silence was broken only by the far-off cry of a bittern as the group fixed their attention on his words.

"Though I walk through the valley of the shadow of death…"

Like an echo, the Gaelic he'd heard at his mother's knee kept time with the English translation.

"Thou preparest a table before me in the presence of mine enemies…"

The words pricked at his soul.

"Surely goodness and lovingkindness shall follow me…"

Lovingkindness… *tròcair*—mercy. A loving, compassionate mercy.

He finished the psalm. He rested his gaze on the shrouded body, humbled in death.

"Henry Jackson believed these things. The Lord was his shepherd. The Lord watched over him with compassionate mercy and care."

Ian's voice cracked. His own words thrust him through like an arrow.

"His last words were, 'Precious in the sight of the Lord is the death of his saints.' What we see as evil may be a mercy."

He couldn't breathe. He looked at Quash, hoping the man would understand.

Quash nodded. "Let us pray."

* * *

IN THE MORNING dimness Iain woke. He'd heard the carriage clattering in the drive well after dark; both master and mistress must have returned.

The cabin was empty, *felt* empty. He glanced at Henry's pallet. Iain had folded several items of clothing Hector might fit into. Joe's shoulders were much too wide. He'd benefit

48

from the blanket. It was a sad chore to give away the man's belongings. But the man would want to bless others.

It still hurt.

Iain shrugged into his work clothes and walked out to the field. There was someone new there.

Joe and Hector were speaking to a wiry young Black man at the edge of the indigo field. The tones of their conversation slowly came clear as Iain approached.

"You be sure?" Joe asked.

"I'm here, ain't I?" the young man said.

"Ain't you a town slave?" This from Hector.

The new man straightened. "Only the cook and Mr. Cartwright are staying in town. The rest of us are coming here."

Mr. Cartwright was the Pinckneys' factor. He'd come a few times to the plantation.

"Why?" Iain asked.

The new man turned and saw him. His face instantly took on a guarded expression.

Hector said, "This here Jabez. He says the master is going to London."

Iain frowned. "The master?"

Jabez examined Ian's clothing, then seemed to relax. "The whole family. All going."

Joe handed Jabez a scythe. "Can't stand here jawin'. Indigo won't cut itself."

Iain grabbed a blade and some twine. "Joe, will ye teach him?"

They split up and bent to their work.

The sun rose steadily and the heavy heat grew. The familiar dampness crept into Iain's shirt as he bent and cut, bent and cut. His mind kept drifting to the news. The Pinckneys leaving... such events always affected the hands.

Would his contract be sold again?

"Mr. Mac! Mr. Mac!" It was Rosey's son, who worked in the stables. Vaguely Iain acknowledged the "Mister" before his name. The acknowledgement of what every slave knew: Iain MacLeod had white skin and would not be in bondage forever.

If he survived this fever-ridden land.

He waited for the lad to get closer and explain himself before putting away his tools. Once the day warmed, extra motion was costly, and every man spent his efforts wisely.

"Mr. Mac! Master wants you! Diablo be sick, kicking his stall!"

Iain moved quickly. Whatever damage had been done had happened yesterday, he was sure. His mind moved over the remedies for a colicky horse. That's what it undoubtedly was. Too much grain, and last night's midnight arrival. He'd received little care.

Even before he arrived at the stables, he heard the trumpeting of an animal in distress. A crash echoed inside.

Mr. Pinckney laid his hand on the stall door, then drew it back again. The stallion, the man's favorite horse, was high strung as it was. Blotches of sweat marked the dark bay's withers as he shifted and stamped.

"Can you help?"

Iain had helped a mare foal a month ago. Gave tips to Rosey's son, who mucked out the stalls and curried the mares and geldings. He was known to be good with animals.

"He needs to walk. And ask Miss—Mrs. Pinckney for chamomile tea. A bucket full."

Iain crooned softly to the horse, waiting for a lull in his nervous pacing and kicking. Then he went into the stall, murmuring and singing a psalm.

Diablo hesitated and flicked an ear toward the sound.

"Let's walk a bit, shall we?"

For hours, Iain walked the horse and gave him chamomile tea. So far, Diablo had only rolled once, the sign of an animal in severe distress.

Iain was hopeful. But colic could kill.

Mr. Pinckney hovered, then went inside, then came back again. "Will he recover?"

"Have ye any turpentine?"

It was difficult to drench a horse, but he'd do it if the tea didn't work.

"I'll fetch it."

In the end, it was not needed. Sometime during the afternoon, Diablo dipped his head and moved his bowels. The crisis was over.

Iain returned the horse to his stall and sat heavily on the mounting block. He was exhausted.

"Mr. MacLeod, come to my study." Mr. Pinckney handed him a tankard of watered ale.

Ian drank greedily and followed the man inside.

* * *

"So you see, Jabez and Mr. Williams will work here." Mr. Pinckney's face twitched. "The house in Charles Town will essentially be closed for the duration."

Iain said nothing, only nodded. The plans of his master were out of his control. He was like a piece of driftwood bobbing on the sea foam.

Mrs. Pinckney had been a friend, of sorts. Now she would be gone.

Mr. Pinckney seemed uncomfortable in the chair behind the desk. "There are several years left on your contract."

Four years and a little over a month remained.

"I promised Mrs. Pinckney I'd find you a good place."

Iain forced himself to breathe.

"I'll advertise you as a groom, good with horses." The fine cravat bobbed as he swallowed. "I am profoundly grateful for your service."

Horses. No more laboring in the fields. He'd be glad to muck out stalls, anything. "I thank ye."

But he'd leave a piece of his heart here. Buried in the graveyard.

CHAPTER 8

THE SHENANDOAH VALLEY

*M*ary set the water bucket down and paused, watching the babies play. Well, they weren't babies anymore, not precisely. They toddled about, playing hide-and-seek or thrusting their plump hands in the dirt. Thomas and Elizabeth were the best of playmates, and Ma minded them during the day while Mary worked, doing the laundry, milking the cows, and cleaning the chicken coop.

She looked beyond the garden to the fields, but she didn't see Simon. Nowadays he worked for the Houstons, and she missed the sight of his strong back. But she saw him at church—kirk, as most called it—and several times he'd come to the Bordens' home on one pretext or another.

Mary emptied the bucket into the big black wash pot over the fire pit and fetched the clothes. The household produced a dozen or so dirty linsey shirts and shifts every week. She didn't mind the work. The children's clothing was positively filthy, and sometimes the strong lye soap proved ineffective. On her mother's advice, she took the items to the stream and pounded the stains with smooth stones. Once, when a blood-stain seemed permanent, she asked her mother about dyeing.

"It'd be better to dye the whole thing red!"

"Aye," Ma said. "Some favor dyed fabric for that reason, but 'tis easy to sew up the plain linsey for everyday clothes. There's a few in the valley who have the knack of dyes."

But she didn't say who.

And there was a more pressing matter to think about. A matter that made her heart race when she did.

Simon. She thought of him by his first name now, though she would never speak it. Thinking of the twinkle in his eye and the single dimple when he smiled made her go trembly inside.

Sometimes, though, that trembly feeling reminded her of Mr. Byrd, and she forced herself to think of something else more pleasant. Like the problem of where to place the chicken manure until it rotted and could be used in the garden. Or the new calf's runny nose.

Today, though, she'd have to face it. Her mother's expres-sion showed that she knew.

"What did Mr. McKee speak to ye about yesterday after meeting?" Ma asked when the laundry was finished.

Sweaty, Mary chose a stool well away from the glowing hearth. A cool breeze wafted in through the open door.

"Ma... he asked me to marry him." There. She'd said it. Words she feared, and yet words that thrilled her heart. This man knew everything—well, he'd known she'd had a child out of wedlock—and still wanted to marry her. It was a puzzle. And a joy.

Ma merely studied her sewing. Her expression showed only mild surprise. As if she expected it.

"Well now, is it what ye want?"

Mary wasn't sure how to answer. It wasn't possible until her contract was fulfilled in the fall. But at that time, she and her mother would both be eligible to own fifty acres of land. A home of their own, and Mr. Borden had mentioned it already. He knew everything about land and deeds.

"The babe needs a name," Mary said. It was a concrete fact, more reliable than her confused feelings. A child born outside of wedlock was born under a cloud. Not to mention the fact that Mary and her mother could not work the land by themselves. A garden, yes, but not fields and fencing. "And ye could live with us." She could provide for her mother.

"Nay. I will stay and work for the Bordens. 'Tis already settled."

"But your fifty acres!"

"I'll ask for a parcel next to yours. We'll use it for wood and foraging, same as here."

One hundred acres of land was a king's portion. A blessing from heaven.

* * *

THE GOLDEN FALL days brought a plentiful harvest. Mary labored past dusk once the corn was ripe, shucking and braiding the ears. Ma worked inside, minding the children or sewing. She always tucked away her needle and thread quickly when Mary came inside.

Simon came to the house once, but he closeted himself with Mr. Borden. Never spoke to her. But behind the meetinghouse one bright Sunday afternoon he'd confirmed the wedding date.

"I bought a horse," he'd said, face glowing. "Fit for saddle and plowing."

Their house would be raised the week before they signed the marriage license. The Bordens, Cunninghams, and Houstons would all pitch in.

"I've felled a dozen trees on that patch of ground," Simon explained. "It's a bonny place, with several large chestnut trees nearby."

Mary loved chestnuts—all nuts, really, and it warmed her heart to know she wouldn't have to go far for them.

Time alternately jumped and crawled as the day appointed drew near. Finally, Mr. Borden came out of his tiny study with a piece of paper. Mrs. Borden did not rise from her seat near the hearth, but a smile flickered on her face.

Little Elizabeth jumped at his knees, knowing something was happening. He handed Mary the paper and picked up his daughter.

"Thank you for your service. I've the deeds in my study, awaiting your signature, yours and your mother's."

Mary scanned the document. Passed hand to hand, it was slightly yellowed and battered around the edges, but very official-looking for all that. *Benjamin Borden* was signed at the bottom, the letters neat and regular, like the man himself.

She ignored the other signatures, the evidence of her life in bondage. But she remembered where she'd signed it herself—she forced herself to look at it now, a thin loopy scrawl near the top.

She'd agreed to it. But it wasn't as if they'd had any choice.

And now it was all over.

Her face seemed to take on a life of its own, a grin spreading wide without conscious thought.

I'm free.

"Mary." Ma's voice trembled slightly. "I've a gift for ye." She stood and held up a gown.

Indigo muslin folds spilled and opened, the hem brushing the floor. Ecru lace trimmed an embroidered stomacher.

"I made a matching petticoat," Ma said.

For a moment Mary's voice caught in her throat. Ma was skilled with the needle and had served the Bordens in that capacity all this time. Mary had glimpsed her working on the petticoat, an old one of Mrs. Borden's, turned and embroidered at the hem. Blue asters and pink lady's slippers. But she hadn't guessed it was for her.

She wasn't worthy of a special wedding gown.

Tears ran down her cheeks. "Ma ..."

"Ye need something bright for the ceilidh after the signing. And ye needed a Sabbath gown anyhow." Her mother looked away.

"I've a gift as well." Mrs. Borden rose and walked to the door, where they all hung their cloaks and coats. She loosed the green plaid cloak and brought it to her.

Her voice was low, gruff. "Take this and wear it with my blessing upon it. And always remember what it means."

Jesus' robe of righteousness.

Her throat closed up, and for a moment she couldn't speak. "Thank ye kindly."

Her heart latched onto that kernel of hope. Jesus' robe to cover her shame. It didn't seem real yet, but maybe one day it would.

The wedding day dawned bright and cheerful. Neighbors arrived on foot, on horseback, and in wagons, their wheels stirring up dust behind them. Mary's heart swelled with gratitude. Even the Houstons had come.

The Cunninghams' spacious barn had been cleared and swept for the occasion. Mrs. Borden was everywhere, directing the women, who seemed to need little supervision —food crowded trestle tables, punch was served, and sweets were handed out to children as if by magic.

Rob Anderson produced his fiddle, and even young Samuel McDowell drew one of his sisters into a reel. The Bowyer brothers led out laughing young women, and Mrs. Borden teased her husband until he joined in, too.

Mary found her feet flying as she danced with her husband in the crowded barn. Simon was smiling, and the world seemed young.

* * *

LATER, Mary couldn't decide when it all started to go wrong. The first days of their marriage glowed bright, when Simon had been patient and never complained, not at burned porridge nor her timidity after dark.

He worked hard. Over the winter he set traps for rabbits and ermine and hired himself out to various families when they needed fences mended or land cleared. At home, he cleared a spot for Mary's garden and labored to prepare a cornfield.

His grumbles seemed minor. Once, tired at the end of a day, he'd said that by all rights her land belonged to him. But Mary dismissed the comment. The fifty acre tract was their home, and what did it matter that her name was on the deed?

The weather turned. For a few days in January they were snowed in. Mary spent the short days mending all Simon's clothes and darning his stockings.

In February they both braved the weather to begin turning up the earth. On sunny days Tommy "helped."

Soon Simon was away more and more, working on neighboring properties. One March day Mary took Tommy to the field. Her job was to gather all the stones and rubbish turned up by the plow. Orange or brown pottery shards made their appearance from time to time, and she shivered when wondering about the people who must have lived here before.

She drew out a potsherd from the plowed earth. "Tommy, look what I found."

He was two years old, and inquisitive. It was difficult to work while minding a young child, and she sought ways to include him.

"Who made this, do ye think? A red Indian?" She handed him the piece of orange pottery, the broken edges worn by time.

Where did these people go?

"I want to play Indian." Tommy threw the shard back into the furrow.

"No, laddie, take it where the others are."

Soon he was piling them into heaps. Another day of this, and she could plant the little garden Simon had cleared. His wages sufficed for seed corn and other essentials.

Then one May evening, Simon returned, with little to show for it but foul breath.

Whiskey. She knew what whiskey smelled like. She'd tasted it before on his lips, but not like this.

He reeked of it. He stumbled and scowled, eyes unfocused. Entering the cabin, he collided with a stool and kicked it aside.

A sudden panic assailed her. She placed her hand over her belly, where she was sure a bairn was started. What would he say if he knew?

A week ago, she would have said he'd rejoice. But now, she feared to tell him.

"What's to eat?" he asked, his glassy eyes falling on her.

This wasn't Simon. This was a stranger.

She opened her mouth to tell him. A rough bread made with cornmeal and ground hickory nuts was all they'd eaten that day. There was still some left. But she never got the chance to speak.

He stumbled noisily to the bed and fell across it fully clothed. His snores began a minute later, and Mary tugged off his boots.

He didn't move.

Sudden loneliness pierced her. There was no one she could tell.

* * *

"Miss Mary, Miss Mary!" The familiar voice was threaded with panic, and Mary opened the door. Young Samuel McDowell hailed her from his perch on a tall black stallion at the edge of the property.

It was Mrs. Borden's stallion Dobbie. She came outside. What was wrong?

"Your ma wants you," said Sammy. "Everyone is sick." He kept the horse at the edge of the clearing, as if afraid to come closer.

"Sick?" Mary gathered her shawl close about her, though summer's warmth had penetrated the morning's brief chill.

Sammy winced. "Smallpox. Have you had it?"

"Aye, but not my son." She suppressed the haunting images that flashed in her mind. "Loan me your horse, and I'll take him to the McClures'. Then I'll come directly."

But it was at that moment that Simon chose to come home, riding the ill-favored bay plow horse. She tensed. The past week he'd been sober, but there was no predicting it. Today, his gaze was steady and he carried a sack over his shoulder, probably part of his payment. She liked it when they were paid in food. She relaxed slightly.

"Ho, what's the news?"

Sammy told him.

A wash of fear traveled over his features. "Stay back."

"I'm going to help the Bordens," Mary said. "I'll ride Dobbie."

Simon's eyes narrowed. "Nay, you will not."

"I'm taking Tommy to Maggie McClure." It wasn't far. "I cannot get the smallpox. I had it when I was young."

She thrust back the images that assailed her mind. The memory was painful.

"Your mother can help."

Fear clutched at her. "Ma was away when Pa got sick. She's never had it. She needs me."

In Ireland, the speckled monster had stripped them of everything they had. When their rent had been raised, the barley and wool they produced on their farm hadn't been sufficient to pay it. Ma had found a position in Baron Cole's household, but she had to live there. When her father and young brother died of smallpox, the position did not pay enough to support them both. They sold their belongings to eat, finally resorting to the indignity of signing indentures.

Mary couldn't stay away. "Maggie will keep Tommy, and I'll be fine. I'll stay there until the sickness is gone."

Quickly, she took the child and led the stallion to the broad stump where Simon chopped their firewood. She used it to mount Dobbie. Horses frightened her, but not today. Smallpox was worse.

Simon's anger rose off him like steam, and he hurled imprecations at Sammy, who ran off through the woods. Mary half-expected Simon to grab the reins and stop her, but he merely scowled.

Clumsily, Mary urged Dobbie forward with one hand on the reins, the other arm like iron about her son. The ground was far away, and her pulse thudded in her ears. But the horse gave her no trouble, and she followed the half-hidden track to the McClures' house.

Lord, have mercy on Ma. Have mercy on the Bordens.

But He hadn't shown mercy to Pa. He hadn't been merciful to her family.

Her hopes shrank.

CHAPTER 9

The smell of freshly turned earth mingled with the dark scent of death. Juniper and cinnamon in the linen winding clothes were no match for the heat of summer, nor the days that had passed as Mary waited with the others for the grim reaper's final tale.

Mr. Borden had died first, and his body now lay in a freshly constructed box that added its own piney scent to the horrible perfume.

The funeral was sparsely attended. The McClures were the last to arrive, their sturdy wagon clattering over the ruts, mules snuffing the wind, nostrils extended.

Mary stood well behind the minister. The Bowyer brothers had come early to dig the graves. Sweat darkened their temples. The patriarch of the Cunninghams presided near the minister, sporting a pockmarked face that declared him to be a veteran of the unseen battle that had just come and gone.

Thankfully, the dread disease had not spread. Mr. Borden

must have caught it on his last trip to the tidewater. The valley was spared.

But a dead, dull blanket oppressed Mary's heart. Everything good, every hope was forgotten, snatched away by the cruel pox.

Two open pits stood ready to receive the three victims. Baby Elizabeth had been placed into her father's coffin. She'd grown cold the day after his battle ended.

Mary finally allowed her gaze to settle on the shrouded form next to the second grave.

Ma.

Her mother had been the last to die. She'd ignored the fever for two days, sponging faces, changing bedding, trying to get Elizabeth to sip broth.

Mrs. Borden recovered after a week. Surely Ma would rally too.

But she hadn't, and now Mary felt thin and ragged, like a sheet washed and pounded and wrung out once too often.

"Ma!" Tommy's voice was a welcome distraction. Maggie McClure relinquished her son into her arms. Mary buried her nose in his hair, grateful for his familiar warmth and scent.

Maggie remained nearby, her presence a vague comfort.

The minister started to speak, but his words ebbed and flowed over her consciousness, their meaning slipping away.

Across the small graveyard, Mrs. Borden sat on a chair someone had brought, and her remaining children gathered round. She was pale. The pustules on her face and neck had dried up, but several small pink marks remained.

She would still be beautiful, unlike some whose abundant pocks disfigured their faces.

The younger children remained close to their mother. James had become very sick but three days ago his fever had broken. Halfway through the sermon, he folded his limbs and sat on the ground, thin and wan.

Mary's knees weakened in sympathy. Last night she'd fallen into a dreamless sleep, only to be wakened at midnight by Martha's whimpering. Sadness marked Sarah's features as she stood behind him. Samuel squared his shoulders once, the man of the house now.

Samuel had escaped the dread illness completely. A strange thing. Ma had explained once that smallpox killed some but barely touched others. Mary had only a few of the marks herself.

Why would a strong, hearty man like her father be felled and she herself spared?

And Mr. Borden. He was not aged. He was a quiet, plain man. More honorable than many in the tidewater, unlike William Byrd—

No, she wouldn't think of *him*.

But why would God take Mr. Borden's life, and her mother's, and Elizabeth's, and spare a man like Mr. Byrd?

It made no sense.

The minister rambled on. He spoke of heaven.

But hope and heaven seemed very far away.

MARY TUGGED a fresh shirt over her son's head. Clean, but stained. No matter. "Let's dig in the dirt, Tommy."

She forced cheerfulness into her voice. The world seemed empty, and the lined crate she used as a pantry was empty too. She had about half a cup of molasses left and perhaps a pint of cornmeal. There was a bit of ham left over from the time Simon had worked for the Houstons, but she was saving that for him.

When he returned. He'd left early that morning without explanation. Was he working… or—

She could not complete the thought.

Her stomach complained as they entered the weedy cornfield. She'd eaten a little, shared the thin cornmeal porridge evenly with Tommy, but what satisfied him was not sufficient for her.

Maybe it was the baby. She frowned and glanced briefly at the gentle curve of her belly. She didn't mind going without, but she had to take thought for the bairn.

She chopped at the stubborn weeds with the hoe for an hour, then stopped and looked at the woods to the east. It was too soon for persimmons or paw paws; perhaps there were still blueberries in the thickets.

Where was the property line? Mr. Borden had given her a general idea last fall. She wanted to go foraging but did not want to trespass.

"Ma! Horsey!" Smudged with dirt, Tommy stood and pointed.

A breeze stirred the cottonwoods along the stream. Like a specter, a dark horse and rider emerged cloaked by the rustling leaves. Stray gusts lifted stray blonde locks of the rider like a cloud.

Mary froze at the otherworldly sight. Then the ghostly rider resolved into the familiar image of Mrs. Borden on Dobbie.

She urged the horse across the summer-shallow creek. A blue-green cloak lay across the saddle.

Had Mary forgotten the cloak at the Bordens' home?

But no, it was safely inside.

"Thomas Kerr has a fine loom." Mrs. Borden must have noticed Mary's gaze. "I directed the design. Agnes May dyed the wool."

"Beautiful."

"You look thin." Mrs. Borden dismounted and tied Dobbie to a sapling in reach of a few thick stands of grass.

Only a month past her illness, Mrs. Borden looked thinner too, but it merely made her more lovely. Her cheekbones were more pronounced, framing her remarkable gray-green eyes. Her hair was still untouched by gray, and the smallpox scars were fading. Surely she would marry again.

In contrast, Mary felt ugly, unwanted. Now even her husband stayed away half the time.

Tommy bounded over and hugged Mrs. Borden's legs.

"I've something for ye, young Thomas." She thrust her hand into her satchel and pulled out a carved toy. "A fine stallion. Sammy carved it."

Tommy collapsed on the ground and began playing with the wooden horse, emitting pleased giggles.

How could she ride all this way after her loss, and remember a child not her own?

"I'm that sorry." The words escaped her lips.

"I willna say it doesna hurt. It does. Every morning when I wake alone. But then I look at the fine children my Lord has left me, and it helps. And I look at the fine colors of the sunrise, and it helps." She pressed a hand to her breast. "But most of all, I look at Christ. His wounds purchased everything I need, both for this life and the next. Aye, I look at Christ, and that helps most of all."

The breeze picked up, sending the cottonwood leaves fluttering.

"I've something for ye," Mrs. Borden continued softly. "Two things. First, the deed to the land. Your mother's land."

Mary had a hazy idea that she'd inherit her mother's fifty acres but did not understand how the process worked.

Mrs. Borden pulled out a folded piece of paper. "Here.

See if this meets with your approval. Then sign, and I'll file it at the courthouse."

The beautiful slanting penmanship of the official document faded away when she saw the name at the center.

Thomas Pickens McKee . . . Her son's name was listed as the new owner. "Tommy?"

"Your ma told me to give it to Tommy. You would manage it until his majority, of course."

Mary frowned. She didn't have pen and ink in the cabin.

"Here." Mrs. Borden pulled out a capped inkwell and a quill from the satchel.

Mary scratched out her signature and handed back the deed. "Thank ye kindly." No matter what she suffered, her son would have a chance.

Mrs. Borden's eyes glistened as she replaced the document. "One more thing." She pulled out a book. "Ye must recognize this."

Ma's Bible.

"Aye." Mary cradled it briefly, then slipped into her apron's pocket. She'd keep it safe. Safe from the rambunctious hands of a toddler—or the unpredictable moods of a husband.

"Mary." Mrs. Borden's eyes were kind. "Ye've good timber on your mother's land. Some longleaf pine, some walnut."

Mary had gathered walnuts last fall. "The largest walnut doesna give much."

"But it's valuable for the wood. Might swap for some things. Ye managed my chickens. I've got a dozen pullets."

Mary nodded. Chickens would help her feed her growing family.

"Mr. Bowyer will see to it." With fluid grace, she mounted Dobbie and disappeared through the cottonwoods.

Mary scanned the property looking for a place to build a chicken coop, her eyes dimmed suddenly by tears.

Thankful, she fingered the Bible in her pocket. Ma's words came to her like a dream, a childhood memory of sitting at her knee sounding out clunky, unfamiliar words. *"You'll be able to read the Scriptures. That's what's important."*

"Yes, Ma," she spoke into the breeze.

* * *

A RUMBLE of creaks and equine complaints alerted Mary to a visitor late the next day.

Simon?

She opened the door. Simon drove the wagon into the yard, the familiar bay gelding harnessed to the ancient vehicle, bags and crates peeping over the sides.

Her husband grinned. "Wilkins shot a deer. I bagged a turkey—which we ate, but he divided up the doe." He nodded toward a large sack next to him on the cart's seat, then hopped down.

"What's all this?"

Peeping sounded from a crate. Tiny bills poked out between the slats—her chicks! A nearby bag wriggled as if alive.

Simon opened the bag and lifted out a puppy. Dangling from the scruff of its neck, the reddish-brown creature waved paws too big for its size. It yelped several times, slobber dripping from its tongue.

What they would feed it? She kept her mouth closed. They'd manage somehow. She laid her hand on the side of the cart and looked inside to find kegs and jugs and a lumpy burlap sack containing either turnips or onions. Her mouth watered. "I'll find a bit of rope for the puppy."

"She'll be protection when I'm away working or hunting."

Tommy jumped at her apron. "Doggie!"

"Bowyer threw in the puppy for nothing. Did I say I made a trade?" He unloaded one of the sacks. "Barley. And salt, sugar, molasses, and vinegar."

Mary tied a rope about the puppy's neck and looped the other end around the hitching post. "No, you didn't. What did you give?"

"Three trees. That's it, three trees. A huge walnut, and some longleaf pine."

He closed the distance between them and drew her to himself. "I know you were worried."

His body was warm, sweaty, and familiar. She smiled.

"John Bowyer told me we have some prime timber, just need to manage it, cut the older trees, leave the younger to grow."

Mary laid her head on his chest. They wouldn't starve this winter. "I've got good news for you, Simon."

He kissed her hair.

"We're having a bairn."

He loosed his grip and scanned her form. "Truly?"

She nodded. Would he be angry?

A smile spread across his face. "I've a jug of cider. Let's celebrate."

Thank you, Lord.

CHAPTER 10

WEST OF THE SHENANDOAH VALLEY, JUNE 1753

*I*ain jolted awake. It was dark. Hickory and ash smoke still filled his nose, evidence that the evening fire still burned. He sought the stars through the branches above, an instinct he retained from the lonely days shepherding sheep on the moor, waiting for the clouds to part and reveal the heavenly time-clock.

Voices rumbled on the other side of the fire. His new master, a Uchee trader with an English name of George, was speaking to the man they were escorting, a chief of some sort. The man came from a different tribe than George did, but Iain was always amazed at the alacrity the trader possessed in communicating to all and sundry. He spoke both English and presumably his own Uchee language fluently, but when meeting up with red men of other tribes he used a general-purpose patois that seemed to cover the basics.

Sometimes Iain could understand it. He'd picked up a few words of Uchee in the three years he'd served the man and could make polite noises in Shawnee, Muskogee, and Catawba. Some English and French words had made their way into the traders' lingo, and using guesswork and context, Ian could often follow a conversation not meant for his ears.

The rumbles resolved into meaning. They were discussing the Shawnee.

"Dangerous for the white one," the chief seemed to say.

White one? Did that mean all white men, or himself in particular? The Shawnee lived west of here, near enough to be a concern to settlers in the backcountry.

George did not sound disposed to argue with the man's point, whatever it was. "I will leave Betsy in the daughter of the stars."

"And the white man?"

But Iain was wrestling with his master's words. Daughter of the stars? He rolled the sounds in his mouth and finally they made sense.

Shen-an-do-ah. The Shenandoah Valley.

A velvet-soft nose connected with his ear, making him jump. It was Betsy, her breath warm against his face. She was the mule under discussion—she was old, too old really to be hauling goods over the mountains. He checked her feet every evening. The other mule, Buck, was more temperamental but younger.

Iain felt for Betsy's halter. "Let's go, Betts. I saw some sweet grass yonder." Reluctantly, he eased himself out of the bed he'd created with leaf litter and a blanket. The conversation behind him stopped while he re-tethered the animal, murmuring all the while to settle her.

The Pinckneys had been kind in finding him a place to

care for animals. But never in his wildest dreams would he have imagined a red man for his master, nor the work that sent him deep into the wilderness, obtaining skins and salt from the Indians in return for the multitude of items they desired: iron kettles, knives, tomahawk heads, colorful shirts, mirrors, and beads.

They never traded in muskets or ammunition. George had explained that it was too dangerous. White men objected, and muskets were so coveted they could cause disputes in the villages. He also did not sell whiskey.

"I care for my people," he had said, without further explanation.

Iain found his bed again, and his eyelids grew heavy.

The daughter of the stars. He slept.

* * *

SEVERAL DAYS LATER, the path grew steep and difficult. Iain stumbled, a rivulet of sweat running into his eye. He scrambled to his feet and wiped his face with his sleeve. The trail here was not much more than a deer track, and both the rocky ground and the trees fought him. He was grateful when George called a halt and led them to a tiny hidden spring. Buck bugled his approval with a noisy series of brays, then nosed Betsy out of the way in his rush for the water.

Iain was too tired to scold. He sat on a half-crumbled log and opened his canteen, poured its contents down his throat, then rose to fill it from the spring.

George handed him a strip of jerky. "If'n you look through those trees yonder, you can see the valley."

Iain thrust the meat in his mouth and maneuvered for a better view. An opening in the foliage revealed a distant ridge. They had reached the top of the Gap.

"Blue Ridge Mountains, 'bout thirty mile or so." George took a bite, chewed, then swallowed. "Staunton is my first stop, the main town."

This was unusual. George dressed as a white man, but even so, he tended to avoid settlements. Trading posts were safer, where everyone expected to see Indians.

"I've been there before. A few know me." He fixed his gaze squarely on Iain. "A few I trust."

They finished their meal. The chief had slipped off, as he sometimes did, possibly checking for pursuit. They'd been traveling through a disputed region, with Cherokee, Shawnee, and white settlers a little too close for comfort, and now George was taking the chief all the way to the Virginia coast. They would encounter hostile faces all the way.

To Iain's mind, he'd be of the greatest use to the trader east of the Blue Ridge mountains, where a white face would be a help. But he'd known for several days, ever since that evening conversation, that change was ahead.

He waited for the trader to continue.

"Trouble is coming. Like the red sky at sunset, the Great Spirit gives a sign. It will not be safe for you in the mountains anymore."

The Shawnee. It had to concern the Shawnee. Even though he'd heard French names woven in the patois of the trader, the French were far to the north.

The chief slipped around a rhododendron thicket and found his way to them. Iain dived for the mules' ropes but George held up a hand.

"You have one year left on your contract," he said bluntly. "I will give you a choice. I trust three men in the valley. McClure, Houston, and Russell."

The why of it no longer mattered. The choice was before him.

And the choice was his, a strange but refreshing notion.

* * *

THEY MADE it to Staunton the next day and did not stay long. George seemed tense and kept up a steady pace, and by noon Iain began to check Betsy's feet. The path they were taking led to a beautiful, rippling tributary of the Shenandoah. The Russells' homestead was near—George was almost sure of the way.

The path beside the river was shady and peaceful. The chief walked just behind the trader's tall form and Ian trailed, minding the beasts. After an hour, red flashed ahead through the gaps in the summer foliage.

Iain wiped the sweat out of his eyes and blinked. Friend or foe?

A girl came into view, standing in the shallows of the river. She wore a madder-red skirt, and her dark hair was uncovered. Tall and vigorous, she wrestled with a fishing pole curving beneath the weight of a fish. Then the chief skirted a sapling and blocked Ian's view of the riverside.

Voices rumbled, George's and the girl's. Just then Buck planted his feet, and Ian clucked at him, grabbing the halter under the plaited strap he'd looped over the stubborn creature's nose. The mule rolled his eyes at the pressure but obeyed.

Leading the animals closer to the voices, Iain could now make out the subject of discussion, a large fish which flapped wildly on the bank.

A bass, by the looks of it. George knocked its head on a rock and pulled out a knife to dress it.

The girl—young woman, rather—was younger than he. Her brown eyes were fixed on the chief, her expression frozen, as if fearful but unwilling to admit it. Iain's mouth twitched a smile. A steady girl.

George finished the task and introduced them all.

"Iain MacLeod."

He heard his name in a daze as he stared. He hadn't seen a young woman—a young *white* woman—in a while.

The cheerful lilt of Scotland was in her voice, and her name was Susanna. She was a Russell, and she agreed to take them to her home.

Iain's heart rate quickened as he followed the others along a path through the trees and fields, aware of the unseen Blue Ridge ahead. The ground began to rise as they passed a small apple orchard to the left. They entered a cleared knoll with a cabin, but they passed the structure and followed the girl to a two-story house partially sided with longleaf planks.

The faint scent of manure signaled horses ahead. Betsy hee-hawed a greeting to the unseen animals.

A lad emerged from the house—about eight or ten, with chestnut hair and bright blue eyes. A man followed, a taller version of the lad, with slightly darker hair.

"Welcome. John Russell, at your service."

George nodded his thanks and introduced them. Hope swelled in Iain's chest, competing with wariness. People were rarely what they seemed. Even the good ones could cause harm without meaning to.

"My son Jonathan will assist Mr. MacLeod with his animals."

"Come ben," sang a Highland voice in welcome. In the doorway, a gray-haired woman beckoned to the visitors to come inside. Tears sprang to Iain's eyes and he blinked furiously, hearing her accent.

Surely he wasn't homesick—not after all this time. He turned from her and followed the lad to a barn.

Entering, Iain savored the warm smells of horse and hay and leather. A single animal poked her head out of a stall and regarded him with a large, intelligent eye.

"That's Percy—actually her name is Perseverance." The lad's chest swelled with pride. "The others are out to pasture."

"A fine-looking mare. A pacer?"

"Ye ken horses?"

"Aye. And sheep." Ian found he couldn't say more, even to a wee lad. He couldn't think of sheep without thinking of the moors of Raasay, purple with summer heather.

"Are you a Highlander like the Mays?" Jonathan grabbed two buckets and seemed poised to fetch water.

Iain swallowed. "From Raasay. An isle near Skye."

A tiny line appeared on the lad's forehead. "Is that near Ireland? My grandda was a schoolteacher in Ireland."

Iain tried to answer in a way the lad could understand. "Not exactly. But my grandmother was a Presbyterian, same as your folks."

There was no time for the convoluted history of the Scottish people, of which the child probably knew little.

Jonathan brightened and dashed off to fill his buckets. When he returned, Iain was almost finished unloading the mules.

"This is Buck." He indicated the darker animal. "Mind him. He's moody. He'll bite without much warning."

Mules, like people, had their reasons, and sometimes they weren't good ones. But at least mules possessed no pretense.

Jonathan gave both animals a wide berth as he filled their troughs with hay. "Let's go inside."

It was obvious the lad was keen to hear the adults'

conversations and goggle at a "real" Indian. George had dark eyes and hair, but once they heard his speech, most back-country folks forgot he was not white. The chief, ornamented with feathers and copper jewelry, was another thing.

John Russell was still speaking to George before the door of the house.

Russell's gaze shifted to Iain. "Mules settled?"

"Aye. Thank ye kindly."

For a moment Russell was silent. He seemed a strong man of mature years, but his hair was untouched by silver. His face looked kindly, thoughtful, but it was marked with several thin white scars.

The man had known trouble. For some reason this eased Iain's mind.

"George wants a home for Betsy," Russell said.

Iain nodded. "She's old, but good-tempered."

"He tells me he's loath to take ye back across the mountains."

Iain fumbled for a way to answer this, but the man continued.

"He's offered me the rest of your contract. I can use a man ready with horses and sheep. Ye ken sheep?"

"Aye, I minded them in Scotland as a lad. Sheared them one season." Shearing was messy, slippery work, and Iain's father waited until he was tall and strong enough to wrestle a ewe into submission. But then the Bonnie Prince had destroyed all that.

Or Cumberland had. He wasn't sure whom to blame more, the wicked duke, or the prince who fled when the battle was lost.

"Then I have but one question. Are ye willing?"

It was his choice. Iain thought of Percy's sweet face, the lad Jonathan, and considered.

"Aye and cider!" The old Highland woman peered out the door.

Hearing her voice caused his throat to constrict. Iain made his decision. He'd stay.

It wasn't Raasay. But maybe it could be a new home.

CHAPTER 11

The house embraced Iain like a warm woolen cloak. The tantalizing aroma of sizzling bacon and baking bread and the tiny clinks of cups and tankards underscored the hearty greetings and kind remarks that filled the space.

The Russell home was sturdy and well-crafted, with a large, fine hearth and a beautiful walnut kitchen table, adorned with the little scars and scratches that spoke of use.

People poured inside, and Iain couldn't keep their names straight, except for Arch May's, a vigorous man with salt-and-pepper hair and a booming Highland voice.

"Sit here, lad." May slapped his back. "Miss Susanna, might he have some ale?"

A pewter tankard slid before him on the table. The dark-haired lass poured it full of the aromatic beverage.

"Thank ye kindly," Iain said to her. Susanna was taller than her mother, whom she resembled not at all. The matriarch of the family was blonde under her mobcap, calm and sharp-eyed, handing off tankards and earthenware cups to her daughter to distribute and fill.

Iain curled his hands around his tankard and looked about. Jonathan crouched in the corner with another child—younger, by the looks of him, with red-gold hair. Their wide-eyed gazes were fixed on George and the chief, who now sat at the head of the table. The whimpers of a younger bairn were silenced by Mrs. Russell, who scooped up the babe and went into the other room.

John Russell welcomed his guests and proceeded with the banter Iain knew so well from his travels, casual inquiries into the health and well-being of their families. Those the white men called savages had a code of civility as complex as any in Charles Town. George translated for the chief. Iain suspected that he wasn't quite as fluent in the Catawba language as all that, but the trader understood the chief's mind and goals, which helped.

Iain sipped his ale and allowed his muscles to relax in the heat of the hearth and the bodies crammed around the table. One wall of this space—a combination kitchen and casual living area—was paneled. A door led to another room, presumably a bedroom or parlor. A single wolf skin adorned the wall across from him.

This was a homestead carved from the wilderness with sweat and toil, but not the sweat and toil of slaves.

"George, Colonel Ayres has been in negotiation with the Iroquois?" John Russell asked. The chief was known by this name among the white men, and served as a sort of emissary on occasion. That much Iain knew.

But the Iroquois? The bits and pieces of conversation he'd overheard mentioned them, but Ian had never managed to figure out whether the subject of the Six Nations referred to a threat or a treaty.

"Yes, and I do know it sounds like the craziest thing," George replied. "In fact, I'm escorting Colonel Ayres to Williamsburg, where he will catch a packet north. The treaty is still being finalized."

A treaty? Between the Catawba and the Iroquois confederation? The men around the table were clearly surprised too.

George attempted an explanation. "The Catawba have a good reason." He paused and spoke to the chief, who responded in the familiar Catawba tongue, showing emotion for the first time, his dark eyes flashing.

The trader gave the sense. "The French want the land to the north and west. They use no chains—he means surveying —but they want all the trade."

A chill prickled along the back of Iain's neck. *The French... the Shawnee...*

A shadow blocked the doorway. A young man.

Beside him, Arch May tensed briefly. "Och, it's only Jamie."

A lanky lad—he seemed no older than Susanna—entered at Russell's command, blond unruly hair brushing the lintel. One cheek was marked with smudges and scrapes. Hesitantly, Jamie joined them, and Susanna handed him an earthenware mug. No one asked about the scrape.

The conversation continued.

"The Six Nations," George said, "especially the Mohawk, are inclined to side with the English. If the Seneca trade with the French, well, that's not necessarily an alliance."

Each tribe looked out for its own interests in the matter of alliances. But what did this have to do with the Catawba?

John Russell asked his daughter to fetch a book, and she brought a fine volume of geography from the other room.

Ian couldn't see the pages Russell was showing George and the chief, both of whom seemed delighted at the maps.

"Here's the Blue Ridge." Russell pointed, then swept his hand along to indicate the coastal cities. "Williamsburg… Philadelphia… Boston."

The chief's brows drew close in concentration, the feather in his hair swinging.

"Here's Quebec and the French forts and trading posts, all along here to the west and the wee settlement at the mouth of the river." Russell's finger followed his words, and Iain tried to imagine it. He only had a vague notion of the areas the French dominated.

Russell straightened. "Ask Colonel Ayres two questions, if ye please. First, what will happen if the French go to war with us, and second, why is he treating with the Iroquois?"

The chief glanced briefly at the face of each man and then replied. George translated. "The French have few warriors here, and you know that much already. However, many Indians are friendly with the French, and would fight on their behalf if asked—and they will ask. The Indians will become their army."

Sudden silence chilled the room. Iain's belly soured. The fragments of conversation he'd heard on the trail fit together now. Maybe not all of the Iroquois confederation would go on the warpath. Even if only the Mohawk did, it would be bad news up north.

The chief continued. "Every white man's hand will turn against the red man. If the Catawba are not clearly in league with the English, we will be regarded as the enemy."

A ginger-haired man across the table spoke. "What of the Shawnee?"

The Shawnee lived just west of here and would be the greatest potential threat to these people.

Next to him, Arch May cleared his throat. "The Shawnee have grievances with everybody."

George tapped his fingers on the map. "They have been pushed around for many years. First by the Six Nations, and now white surveyors cross the Alleghenies."

The chief rumbled in his language, and the trader nodded before translating. "The Shawnee have been patient. They tend their crops, they hunt the deer. But when they go on the warpath, they are fierce fighters. We know. They have Catawba scalps, and we have theirs."

A bairn cried from somewhere.

"And ye think there will be war." Russell's words sliced through the room.

George nodded. "I may not be back very often. Not until things settle." He conferred with the chief. "He says all nations, not just the Catawba, will avoid the great valley. All fear the Shawnee."

Iain had supposed this homestead to be safe. Perhaps it was only a matter of degree.

"Mr. Russell?" Jamie spoke for the first time, his gray-blue eyes bright with intelligence. "I-I ran up the slope and fell into a cavern."

That explained the scrape—and the dirt.

Arch May set down his tankard. "A cavern? A cave?"

"It's very large. A hidey-hole."

John Russell stared at the lad. "Where is it?"

A well-built home was not necessarily a safe refuge. Indians sometimes set buildings on fire.

But a cave—a cavern—could not burn.

* * *

IAIN FOLLOWED the Russells into the log meetinghouse. Henry Jackson had been dead for several years, but his face and winsome speech came to him now seeing the church. Presbyterians called their assembly a "kirk," or church, but the building where they met was merely a large, long cabin. No special windows or decorations. No candles.

He cast his gaze over the benches lined in long rows, some already filled with people. His mind flashed back to the nave of the Inverness kirk, the blood and suffering in the darkness. The pistol shots cutting short the lives of his countrymen outside.

No, perhaps buildings were not holy—if anything was holy.

He tightened his grip on the book in his hand. These Scriptures were holy if anything was. No confusion there.

Iain followed the Russells to a row and sat on the very end. Arch and Agnes May sat across the aisle to his left. This structure, much like the Russells' home, was constructed with some care; the chinking was tight, and the wall behind the minister was paneled with pine.

While waiting for the service to begin, he allowed his mind to drift to the startling discovery two days before.

The cavern.

For cavern it was, not just a dirty cave. A thick rope allowed them to descend easily to the bottom of a large, cool space. Torchlight flashed upon fantastical stones, hanging from the ceiling or projecting from the floor, bright white or yellow or rose, gleaming like the marble he'd seen in the Pinckneys' grand home.

Except that these great pillars of the earth seemed alive, rippling with color. For long minutes he stood silent, frozen to the spot, while the men of Russell's Ridge made comments about water and shelter and supplies.

And Indians.

Indian raids were sudden. Iain understood the way of the red men on the warpath, even if he had never seen it himself. He'd heard enough with George as they went from village to village. More than once an old crone had tugged at his tawny locks in some kind of morbid jest. George said little. He didn't have to. Warriors bore lances decorated with hairy scalps. Most scalps were black. Scalps taken from neighboring tribes.

Once Ian spotted a nut-brown scalp, and the bile had risen in his throat.

The need for a safe hideout was plain. Once he climbed the rope out of the cave into the summer warmth, he memorized the spot.

"O God, our help in ages past, our hope for years to come…"

The singing swelled around him, filling the building. They sang by line, and so Iain was able to join in after a time.

The first song was a psalm fit to meter, the lyrics preserving the sense in a sure poetic beauty. From a psalter, no doubt. The only psalter he knew was the Gaelic, but this felt the same, and something inside him melted.

The minister, a wiry blond man dressed in a plain coat, opened his Bible. His earnest blue gaze swept over the congregation for a moment before he spoke.

"My text furnishes me with proper materials for my purpose. Let heaven and earth hear it with wonder, joy, and raptures of praise. 'God so loved the world, that he gave his only begotten Son, that whoever, or that every one that believes in him should not perish but have everlasting life.'"

God so loved the world . . .

The notion grated on Iain's ears, so contrary to all his experience. What could this verse possibly mean?

Over the next hour, hope fought with guilt as Iain wrestled with the minister's words.

He followed the others out of the building, confused but hopeful. Henry Jackson's notion of grace was here, being preached by the minister. If only he could fully grasp it. If only he could ask questions without being mocked as a papist.

Three feet away, Arch May greeted a neighbor.

Arch May, the Highlander.

Ian knew whom to ask.

CHAPTER 12

APRIL 1754

*T*ommy was crankit. "But I want Daisy."

"Come up, lad." Maggie McClure opened her arms, and Tommy was coaxed into the wagon bed. "The pup will be happier at home."

They were all crankit, Mary decided. Little Joanie was restless, her first tooth hard under her gums.

And Simon was nowhere to be found. He'd announced he'd be selling firewood but hadn't returned in three days. Last fall's bounty had evaporated over the winter, and the pantry was nearly bare. Spring was a hungry time.

The trees were waking from their dormancy, splashes of vibrant green surrounding the cabin, but her heart was still winter dark. Each day she forced herself to take each action —cooking the scraps of food, working in the garden. Alone.

If Simon didn't plow soon there would be no corn crop.

Mary handed the babe to Maggie and climbed onto the

wagon seat beside her, her cloak flapping open and her sleeve slipping up to reveal her forearm.

"What happened to ye?" Maggie returned little Joan, and Samuel slapped the reins against the rumps of the mules. The wagon jolted forward.

Mary tugged the sleeve down and arranged her cloak about her. "Th-the door. It slammed on my arm. Wind caught it."

She kept her voice down. It wouldn't do for Samuel McClure to know. For a woman to guess was one thing. Simon wasn't an evil man; it was just the drink. And in truth, sometimes it *was* her fault. She shouldn't complain about the fallow field or her need for seed for the garden.

The bruise was already turning. The sequence of colors was familiar: purple, then green, then yellow. It would be gone soon; she merely had to keep her sleeve in place, and no one would know.

Joan settled in her arms as the wagon bounced along. In a few minutes she was asleep, soothed by the rocking.

They were going to a funeral.

"How did it happen?" Mary knew only that John Houston had died. It would be a well-attended service; he was one of the original settlers of the valley and an influential member of the meetinghouse she'd attended while serving the Bordens.

"Tree fell on him." Samuel McClure's voice rumbled suddenly. "He was clearing a field, set a tree on fire—"

"He has servants," Maggie broke in, "why he had to clear the field himself ..."

Mary pictured the man, hale and sturdy despite the silver in his hair, refusing to allow indentures or slaves to do all his labor.

"Idiot man." Mr. McClure's voice was suspiciously raspy. "Should have let his men do it."

Mary sorrowed for his wife. At least Margaret Houston had several strong sons and daughters. She would not be alone, nor wanting for anything.

Still, even a full pantry would not make up for lonely nights in a cold bed.

* * *

IAIN JOINED Arch on the wagon seat. Mrs. May would not be going to the funeral.

"Take this." She handed them a large basket, and Iain set it behind them in the wagon bed. It was heavy, and he could smell bridies, the little meat pies Agnes May made of every sort of game: rabbit, turkey, venison, even bear. The Russells, John and his cousin Roy, had brought down a large black bear last fall. They'd eaten bear in stews and pies for weeks. There was still bear jerky in the Mays' pantry.

Were the pies venison or pork? Both sounded marvelous. His stomach rumbled despite the porridge he'd eaten at dawn, just an hour ago.

"Mr. Russell will bring the cider." Mrs. May wiped her face. "Get ye gone." She turned and marched inside the cabin.

Having lived with the older couple for nearly a year, Iain could read her mood. She was heartbroken but refused to show it.

Arch turned the mules and the wagon wheels rattled on the ruts in the path.

They were going to John Houston's funeral.

I trust three men in the valley. McClure, Houston, and Russell.

This Houston who had died in a tragic accident just

yesterday must be one of the trusted men. From the bits and pieces Ian had heard, John Houston was the patriarch of the Houston clan, one of the original settlers of the valley come from Ireland.

Of course, they were all Scots. But not all Scots were the same. Highlanders, Lowlanders, and those who emigrated from Northern Ireland, all had their differences. Here in the valley, those differences remained. To a point.

Arch and Agnes May were Highlanders working for Ulster Scots. It was a strange situation. He knew them to be originally Catholic, but they attended the Tinkling Springs meetinghouse.

Iain had said little at first. He watched. He listened. The Russells were good people, but all his masters had been good people. It hadn't helped much. At least his indenture would be fulfilled in mere months.

He'd be free. But free to do what?

"Mr. May," he ventured after a while. He'd been meaning to ask his questions for a long time. "H-how do ye manage it? I ken ye are Catholic."

Arch cut him a friendly glance. "The meetinghouse? How do I tolerate Presbyterians, is that it?"

"Aye."

Arch seemed to study the mules. "A long story."

Some of the Mays' story Ian knew. The daughter who'd married in Scotland, the son lost to fever in Pennsylvania. The indenture to the elder Russell, known to all as "Grandda." Arch May's present role was as factor, or manager, of John Russell's property, two hundred acres that ran from the base of the Blue Ridge to the river beneath. Pine and oak and walnut, a small apple orchard tended by the Mays, chicken and a couple head of cattle, and best of all, fine horses and sheep.

But these were external things.

"Ye want to know what I think of the preaching."

"Aye." Iain knew there were no priests in Virginia, and only a few in Maryland. There was no way a Catholic could practice his faith properly here.

"Perhaps a better question is what I think of Christ." Arch ran his hand over his short beard. "At first the preaching seemed a bit strange to my ears. Then I realized it was all from the Scriptures, and I knew they were true, so I kept listening. I soon realized that there was a great gulf between me and God."

The man was quiet as he directed the mules into a tiny creek and up the other bank. The jolting of the wagon eased. The trees thinned out, and a great swell of grass rose to either side of the narrow road.

"I lived that way for a while, listening, but putting off dealing with it. Then one Sabbath the preaching pierced my heart, like a nail through butter. I couldna resist. I went to the woods, determined I would not return until I had peace with God."

Henry Jackson'd had that peace.

"Ye didna ask for that story, I ken that, but ye'll understand when I say that the main thing is Christ. He is our peace. His blood was shed for our sins. He is our rock, our hiding place from the wrath of God. And all the rest of it—what clothes the minister wears, none of it matters. Only Christ and His love for sinners. Ye can call yourself Catholic or Protestant, Anglican or Presbyterian, that doesna matter. Only what ye think of Christ."

It was the longest speech Iain had heard Arch make.

* * *

ARCH KEPT the mules to a steady pace, and they arrived at a modest church building well before noon. It was much like Tinkling Springs, but the log walls were half covered by stone. More stone lay piled to one side. Men, women, and children swarmed about, conversing. It could have been any Sabbath meeting except that the mood was vaguely subdued.

Ian couldn't put his finger on it at first. Then he realized. Only the bairns were laughing, and they were quickly shushed.

"Arch May!" A sturdy woman swept toward their wagon. "Where's Agnes?"

The woman was familiar. Maggie—Maggie McClure. A shopkeeper and midwife.

"Stayed to home. The Russells should be here soon."

Several other families from the Staunton area were here as well, a sign of how esteemed Houston was. But Iain didn't recognize the comely young woman near the McClures' wagon. She had a babe in arms, and another bairn clutched at her skirts. Then she turned slightly, and the blue-green of her cloak resolved into the Campbell tartan.

A fierce heat flooded Iain's face. *Campbell.* The colors of the traitor. He fought the emotion—Culloden was eight years past, and an ocean away.

This woman had nothing to do with it.

Arch May eyed him. "Haven't seen the McKees is a good while. Not at meeting."

Iain found no response. The woman turned and looked at him. She was comely—and married.

Arch made a hum in his throat. "I wonder if Mrs. Bowyer gave her that cloak—she's a Campbell. Relation of the laird."

"The Mays are Clan MacDonald," Ian probed.

"My father fought for the laird at Sheriffmuir, that's so."

"Against the Campbells." The 1715 rising for James, the

rightful King of Britain, had come to a halt with that battle. The Campbells' fault then, and also at Culloden much later.

Arch smiled grimly. "Against Mrs. Bowyer's uncle, if I have it right." His expression cleared. "But what has that to do with us, lad? We invent our own feuds here in the valley, and at the moment, the only real danger is from the Shawnee."

Iain flushed with sudden shame. Arch was right. Scotland was a lifetime ago.

* * *

MARY RECOGNIZED some of the members of the Tinkling Springs meetinghouse. The sheriff was here, a tall, dark man with a silver beard. Others were strange to her. Between Simon's disappearances and his overall reluctance to come, they had attended Sabbath meetings only a couple of times.

She minded Tommy, finding his wandering an excuse to stay away from the knots of women quietly conversing. Joanie slept in her arms.

Finally, the crowd moved by some unspoken command into the cemetery, a small area defined by the low stone wall. The minister spoke briefly, then the coffin was lowered, and everyone filed past and dropped a handful of dirt into the grave.

Feeling awkward, Mary backed out of the space. The baby was stirring, and she needed to find a place to feed her.

She bumped into someone and turned.

"Sorry, ma'am." A young man with hair the color of ale doffed his hat in apology.

Mary skittered back. "Nay, I'm sorry, 'twas my fault."

Joanie gave a full-throated wail.

The young man's brows drew together. "The Russells' wagon is right here."

Was her need that obvious?

He guided her to a wagon with an oilskin tarp curving over it, serving as a cover.

"Might I help you?" A blonde woman with a toddler clutching at her skirts stood nearby.

Mary relaxed. "Thank you kindly."

Shared motherhood made the introductions easy. The woman's name was Abigail Russell, and the bairn was Hannah. Mrs. Russell helped her inside and produced several cold meat pies, small enough to fit in the hand. Scottish bridies.

Mary's stomach rumbled. She'd eaten nothing that day and knew her milk suffered when that happened. Abigail passed one to Mary and shared the other with little Hannah.

"Thank you." Mary wished she could express her true gratitude without sounding foolish.

Mrs. Russell smiled. The inside of the wagon was a comfortable place, and Mary's muscles relaxed.

Rumbles from outside the wagon revealed the location of men conversing.

"What have you heard, Russell?"

"About the Indians? Nothing—except that Trader George willna be back anytime soon."

"I don't like it. When a half-breed like him is nervous, we should all be nervous."

"The French are my worry. Governor Dinwiddie sent someone to tell them not to encroach on our land, and they laughed in his face."

The voices faded. Mary fastened her bodice and slid out of the wagon, Joanie sleeping, a smear of milk on her contented lips.

She turned. "Thank you, Mrs. Russell."

"Where do you live?"

"Near the McClures' place."

Abigail nodded. "You are welcome to visit Russell's Ridge any time. 'Tis not far."

Mary nodded, knowing it would never happen. Simon would object, for one thing. It was hard enough keeping him happy.

The murmur of conversation floated over the air as she made her way to the McClures' wagon. Samuel McClure was leaving the cemetery, Tommy asleep on his meaty shoulder. Maggie would be somewhere close by.

The sound of muffled hoofbeats on grass made her turn.

It was Simon, leading the horse. Despite a faint hint of whiskey in the air, he didn't seem drunk. His gaze darted nervously over the crowd.

"Stay away from the Russells," he said.

The Russells were generous people. But Simon hated charity. Mary nodded, but something in her heart hardened in that moment.

She would seek out the Russells if her children were in need.

She wasn't too proud to beg. She'd bear Simon's anger. And the bruises would fade.

CHAPTER 13

*I*ain lunged for the lamb, but its hooves slipped away from his outstretched fingers. Bleating piteously, the animal tumbled over the outcrop and ended up pinned in a narrow crevasse.

The lamb's mother, a slow, fat ewe named Penny, stopped and raised her head toward the sound. The rest of the small flock continued their upward bound through the brush and around the trees, having been startled by a bobcat.

Where was the ram? Iain half hoped Samson had gone after the bobcat, but if so, well—bobcats weren't painters, but they were still dangerous.

"Ho, there, momma, we'll get your bairn back." He crawled over the top of the outcrop and reached toward the lamb.

The bleats continued.

A little closer... *there.* Iain pulled on the front legs, and soon the lamb was free. It bounded to its mother and nosed her flank, seeking comfort.

The sight of the ewe and lamb filled Ian with warmth.

Sheep were familiar and the work a balm to his soul. Despite bobcats, and despite rumors about the French.

The French. They'd promised the prince aid and never came through. In a way, it was a worse betrayal than the Campbells' choice to back the Hanover imposter. The Campbells, at the least, were not liars.

The old bitterness failed to stir him for once. But the French were dangerous—here and now.

A twig snapped below the outcrop.

"The ram working out?" John Russell said. "Thought I noticed a bit of a kerfuffle."

"Bobcat. Dinna think it got anything. Samson may have gone after it."

In the light of the late afternoon sun, Russell's face was streaked with sweat. "Just got back from the minister's house, got half of the siding done." He climbed onto the outcrop and sat. "Went to the courthouse yesterday. Ye're due fifty acres now your contract is up."

Iain's throat closed. Land. He was still an exile, but land of his own sweetened the ache. "Thank ye kindly."

"I'll show ye a likely piece in a day or two." He paused. "Down at the Craigs' a rider stopped by with news. Said there's been a battle—the French skirmished with the Virginia militia. The governor's man, Washington, lost the battle and had to flee. Indians assisted the French troops in looting what they were forced to leave behind."

The hair rose on Iain's neck. "Indians? Are all Indians allied with the French?"

"I dinna believe so. But ye remember what the Catawba chief said. The Indians are natural allies with the French. They see the French as traders, not settlers that push them out of their hunting grounds."

"What does this mean?"

"I dinna ken. We'll pray and walk canny. We are safe for the moment, but if that should change, I'll send my family east of the Blue Ridge."

The sun went behind a cloud, and Iain shivered despite the heat.

Russell was right to take precautions.

* * *

MARY SAVORED A SINGLE BLUEBERRY, the swell of sweetness filling her mouth with water. At her side, Tommy grinned, half his face purple. Even Joanie had gummed a few berries—a good thing, as Mary's milk was drying up. Only a few blueberries actually made it into the basket in her son's hand.

She shifted Joanie to her other arm and directed them toward the cabin. Hungry, the hour of foraging had worn her out. She hadn't been able to cook a hearty meal in a week. The last of the venison Simon had brought home she'd given him three days ago.

The corn was high, what there was of it. Soon Simon would harvest some of the tender ears, and they'd leave the rest to dry for the winter's cornmeal. Meanwhile, they needed to eat. The stream—they could fish. But the stream yielded little, mainly tiny sunfish. Just beyond her property, the South River flowed, teeming with trout—but would it be trespassing to go there? She didn't know who owned the tract where their stream poured into the river.

Barking signaled a visitor—at least, she hoped. Mary had heard the scream of a painter cat one lonely evening and always took a big stick with her when going into the woods. She slowed as she drew near.

Through the trees, she glimpsed a wagon. Blond hair under a cap—Abigail Russell?

"Hello, have you been waiting long?" Mary asked.

Smiling, Mrs. Russell shook her head. "Have you met my daughter Susanna?"

A tall brunette circled the horses with a large basket hooked over her arm. "Pleased to meet ye."

"Come inside." Mary gestured. "I need to wipe Tommy's face."

"Here, let me help," Mrs. Russell said, opening her arms to take Joanie.

Soon they were sitting around the rickety table sipping acorn coffee.

"I'd like to invite you to the Ridge. Maggie too, she's always a welcome visitor. Either before harvest or afterward, you know how it can be during."

Mrs. Russell's kind words warmed Mary's insides.

Susanna reached into the basket at her feet. "My uncle tans hides and makes things of leather." She drew out two small pairs of shoes. "These are for the bairns."

"Oh." Mary's eyes filled with tears. Tommy needed shoes —and here were warm moccasins for Joan too. "Thank you very much."

Soon the rest of the contents of the basket were on the table—a loaf of wheat bread, butter and jam in small crocks, a large chunk of ham. And wonder of wonders, a box of tea.

The shame of her need washed over Mary, but she pushed it aside. She needed food for the children, and if Simon disapproved, that was too bad. She'd face his anger later. For now, she'd receive this largess.

"Why don't we dig in," Mary said. "Mrs. Russell, won't you ask a blessing over this food?"

The Russells nibbled at small pieces of jam-smeared toast. The bread melted in Mary's mouth, and she was glad to see

Tommy take seconds. After finishing their coffee, her visitors rose to leave.

"Mrs. Russell, I hear the fishing is good along the South River." Mary rose and clutched her apron, not sure how to frame her question. "Who owns the piece of land along the bank? I don't—"

"No one owns the fish," Abigail Russell said.

Susanna's face brightened. "I love to fish." Her gaze fell on Joanie. "And I'm good at minding babes." She cut a glance at her mother, who nodded. "Tomorrow?"

Mary's heart warmed. "I'd love that."

BY THE TIME Simon drove the wagon into the yard, the late afternoon shadows were slanting over the cornfield. Mary greeted him as Daisy barked and whined her welcome.

Simon was red-cheeked and cheerful. Not always a good sign, as drink could cheer him before turning him belligerent. He'd hired himself out for the better part of a week cutting hay and should have garnered some wages.

Hopefully, there was something left.

She took a deep breath. She'd married this man, and she'd be faithful to him. Regardless, she had to find a way to feed her children without him. The chickens were invaluable— she fed her children eggs almost every morning. But a few hogs slaughtered in the fall would give them meat. Would he be open to the suggestion today?

He spotted her and lifted a heavy sack. "Turnips." He twisted and lifted another bag. "Soup bones." He jumped down, thrust his head in the second sack, and waved a bone at the dog.

Daisy jumped and barked, her long legs still ending in

huge puppyish paws. Simon tossed her the treat, and she caught it in the air.

"Poor girl is too thin," he said.

"I've saved some berries for you." Mary dared not include the ham or bread she'd hidden in the lined crate that served as a pantry. He'd be suspicious. "I can fry you up some turnips."

The children had eaten. Joanie was sleeping in her cradle and Tommy was outside with the dog. While Simon ate, she broached the subject. "Perhaps in the spring someone will have piglets for sale," she began.

"Papa, Papa, look!" Tommy bounded inside and pointed to his feet.

Mary tensed. There was no hiding the moccasins.

"I see." Simon's jaw knotted. "Very nice." He turned back to his food, but his dark gaze caught Mary.

"You know how I feel about charity," he said.

It was going to be a difficult night.

But she wouldn't cry out. She didn't want the children to hear.

* * *

IAIN'S EYES became unexpectedly moist as he surveyed the piece of ground before the South River. Knee-high grass covered a natural pasture bounded with cottonwood trees in the distance. Willow, beech, and tulip trees sheltered the river from sight, but the murmur of water over stone could not be hid.

It was peaceful. And he knew enough of farming to understand the value of bottomland.

John Russell broke the silence. "Corn'll grow well here."

"And horses."

Horses were expensive. Breeding them was a rich man's hobby. Well, Russell wasn't precisely wealthy. Perhaps one day Iain would have a mare or two to fatten on this rich grass.

And maybe one day he'd have a wife, although the few times the idea crossed his mind Mrs. McKee's face came to mind.

But she was married.

"Who are my neighbors?" he asked Russell.

"Across the river are the Robinsons." Russell pivoted and pointed to the line of cottonwoods. "Yonder are the McKees. Their piece runs up the hill a fair piece, plenty of good timber, if ye need to buy."

Simon McKee. Iain would prefer to have no dealings with the squint-eyed man with a reputation for drunkenness.

"Now that ye mention it," Russell continued, "my daughter was planning to come out this way to help Mrs. McKee."

He cast Russell an inquiring glance.

"They were going fishing," Russell explained.

He motioned, and they strolled along the riverbank with its unique fragrance—the mossy stench of decaying vegetation, the crisp musty odor of baking stone, the faint scent of tulip tree blossoms. Iain took a step too close to the water and his foot sank in oozing mud. He'd fished in Maryland, on Sabbath day afternoons. He'd have to bring a rod to this place.

"Trout?"

Russell hummed agreement. "And small-mouth bass."

"I remember." The day he'd arrived Susanna had caught one.

"Yonder." Russell pointed.

Susanna was wearing the same red skirt Iain had seen that first day. Another dark head bobbed beyond her.

"Howdy," Russell greeted.

Mary McKee jumped to her feet. Her son looked up but did not lose his hold on a fishing pole.

"Da, dinna scare the fish." Susanna held the McKees' baby. "We've got two trout."

"I caught one," Tommy boasted.

Sure enough, two fat fish lazed unhappily in a big bucket, nose to tail, mouths gaping and fins moving.

"I do hope I am not trespassing." Mrs. McKee's hands tightened on a pole of her own. One wrinkled sleeve exposed a red wrist.

Iain a step forward. Dusky purple spots—the mark of fingers—circled her arm.

Rage swelled in him. What a poor excuse of a man who would beat his wife. What a coward, to do such a thing to the mother of his children.

But all Iain said was, "Come and fish anytime."

He couldn't see a way to help this woman, but one day things might change. Simon McKee had better watch his step.

CHAPTER 14

MARCH 1755

*I*ain buckled the donkey's harness. It was a pony harness, but the jack was large, a hefty creature over twelve hands. Problem was, donkeys weren't shaped like horses, and the collar fit awkwardly.

Arch May grunted. "Roy can fix that."

Roy Russell could do anything with leather. The horses' tack fit well, and he made comfortable moccasins. "Aye." Iain wrapped his neckerchief around one side of the collar, and Arch did the same on the other. "For now I think he'll do."

The task was simple, hauling logs to the half-finished cabin on the piece of ground John Russell had given to him.

"I'd take it as a favor if ye'd take this acre next to the Mays," he'd said after finalizing the paperwork on Iain's fifty acres. "Agnes favors ye as a son, and Arch is no longer young. It would be a comfort to all of us if ye lived near them. And it's a short walk to your own property, forbye."

Upon seeing the spot, Iain concurred. Everyone had pitched in to build the cabin, but news from Williamsburg had brought the project to a crawl. British soldiers had arrived in Virginia to fight the French, and the governor was supporting the effort.

John Russell and James Paxton had joined Washington as aides, and a number of others from the valley, including Simon McKee, had enlisted with the Virginia militia. Russell had made good his promise to see his family safe, sending Susanna to Williamsburg to study French, of all things. And Mrs. Russell had taken the other children to relatives in Richmond.

The remaining men at Russell's Ridge were busy with planting and caring for the animals. Mrs. McKee had been asked to serve as housekeeper.

Did her husband know she'd come to live at Russell's Ridge? He'd see it as charity. Iain heartily approved, as even their dog was too thin. If Simon McKee never returned it would be good riddance.

A wicked thought. He ought not wish evil on the man.

Iain led the donkey to one of the fallen trees, trimmed and prepared, and fastened the harness to it. He guided the animal back up the slope, with Arch minding the log's end, keeping it from snagging on rough spots. After five trips they halted to rest and drink of switchel under the long afternoon shadows.

Swallowing the sour drink, Iain thought about General Braddock and his men. *Redcoats.* Russell and the young Jamie would be fighting alongside them. He wasn't sure he could do that.

Arch took a final swig of his canteen. "Penny for your thoughts?"

"They went to fight the papists." The French were hated because they were Catholics.

"Aye, lad, that they did." Arch wiped his forehead. "Does it trouble ye?"

Iain shrugged. He liked the Russells and most folk here. Didn't want to criticize.

Arch wiped his forehead with the back of his sleeve. "Many valley folks dinna ken why they fear the Pope, not exactly."

"The Mass is illegal."

"Aye, folks fear the Mass. But it has no power, for good or ill, unless you trust in it to save you."

A vision smote Iain with sudden clarity—his mother staying home while his father took him to Mass. A priest came to Raasay once a month, and they never missed. "My mother never attended Mass." Even as the words left his mouth, he understood. His mother trusted in Christ, read the Scriptures. Refused to place her trust in anything else.

"Ye said she was a godly woman."

"Aye, she was that." Iain's thoughts whirled between his mother and his friend Henry Jackson. The truths he heard in the meetinghouse week by week niggled at him. He turned the subject. "Mr. May, tell me about that French fort. They say it's in the wilderness."

British soldiers were hardy and could march for many miles each day. They'd tramped through Scotland's glens and moors. But Iain was familiar with the western mountains, thick with trees and rhododendron. There were places no army could navigate.

"Washington is a surveyor, kens the mountains," Arch mused. "If General Braddock listens—"

The thin scream of a child stopped his words.

Iain launched himself from the log, not bothering to see if

Arch was following. What was the lad's name—Tommy? He ran toward the sound—Russell's property.

As his legs fought for speed, Ian's mind ran through the dangers. Bobcats. Coyotes. Painters. Wolves.

To the side of the path he glimpsed the big chestnut tree that marked the location of the underground cavern, the hidey-hole now disguised by an ingenious cover formed of woven willow and yew.

Indians. Could the Shawnee be on the warpath?

He forced his legs to move faster, thrusting aside the branches tearing at his face.

The house came into view. A child, covered in blood. *Tommy?*

No!

* * *

MARY LURCHED at the sound of her son's cry. Heart thumping, she ran outside. Red covered Tommy's face and clothing—blood?

The sobs dwindled. Approaching, Mary saw where his feet were.

Tommy had fallen into Mrs. May's large dye bucket.

"Thomas Pickens McKee, you're in trouble now." But truthfully, Mary was so relieved she had no notion of punishing him.

"I fell."

"Tell the truth now." Clearly, he'd climbed in.

Mr. MacLeod burst through the trees and thundered to a halt. "The lad safe?"

"Yes, he's a naughty child, got into Mrs. May's madder." The dye needed to be washed off right away. "I need to take him to the stream."

She sensed Mr. MacLeod's gaze on her as she lifted Tommy out of the bucket.

"Allow me," Mr. MacLeod said. "A dunking would be helpful for me too."

Mary swallowed. "That's very kind. Wait, and I'll fetch you some toweling." The water of the stream was cold this time of year. They'd need to dry off quickly.

Her pulse still thumping in her ears, she gathered several yards of thick linen and returned. "Don't let Tommy touch it before he's clean, it'll stain."

She watched them leave, her son bouncing along next to Mr. MacLeod's steady gait. The man had a sure way with horses, and he was gentle with children. But he made her nervous in a way she couldn't pin down.

She inspected the madder bucket, wondering how much damage was done. Orange-red bundles of yarn peeked out of the red liquid. Not good. Half of the dye had been lost.

Mrs. May appeared on the path with a basket over her arm. "How's my madder doing?"

"Tommy got into it, I'm afraid." Mrs. May was a wondrous Highland woman with an amazing assortment of receipts—Boston specialties and German schnitzel among them. "I'm that sorry, he spilled some of it."

Mrs. May peered into the bucket. "No matter. I was planning to finish this batch after supper anyway. Let me put these eggs away and you can help me."

Eggs were abundant now that Mary's chickens had joined the small flock of the other woman. Mrs. May sometimes put half a dozen into a big batch of cornbread, even more into a cake.

Mary fetched clips to pin the wool on the line to dry, and the two women made quick work of rinsing the skeins and pinning them up.

"Ma?" Joanie stood in the doorway of the house, hair tousled from sleep.

"Come, lassie." Mrs. May dipped her hand in her skirt pocket and drew out a toy. John Russell carved toys in the winter months and sold most of them. He reserved a few to entertain his younger daughter, Hannah. Occasionally they found their way into Mrs. May's apron pockets.

Joanie smiled and waddled over. The sight gladdened Mary's heart. Joanie—and Tommy too—were beginning to lose that pinched, pale look. Tommy was still thin, but his limbs were always in motion now. Mary hadn't thought of him as lethargic before, but maybe he had been.

Russell's Ridge was a blessing, a refuge. She missed Simon, but she didn't miss the hunger.

Or the bruises.

"Thank you kindly. I'm sorry about the wool." It hadn't soaked long enough.

"Dinna fash yourself. This is a beautiful color. What would you call it? A pretty salmon. We'll do a batch of indigo tomorrow, I'm thinking."

Mary relaxed, the company of the other woman like a warm fire easing cold limbs. Mr. MacLeod and Tommy returned.

"Thank you, Mr. MacLeod." She took the soiled linen toweling from the man's hands. Tommy was both clean and dry, with only a faint trace of pink remaining at his hairline.

Daisy gave a friendly bark, then sat back, her tongue lolling. Even the dog was losing her gaunt look.

"Iain, would ye holler for Arch?" Mrs. May asked. "We'll eat supper the noo."

Mary was nominally the Russells' housekeeper, but the truth of the matter was, Agnes May ruled Russell's Ridge. Ruled the hearth and kept the men fed. Kept their linens in order. Mary was content to serve under her tutelage, cleaning, washing the clothes, and working in the gardens. Agnes managed an extensive madder patch that didn't require much in the way of upkeep, but her turnips did, and Mary kept an eye out for ways she could help the older woman, whose joints could not be supple.

They went inside and Mrs. May stirred the kettle on the hearth. Mary beat four eggs in a bowl until they foamed, then added milk. Soon a rich cornmeal batter was ready for the pan. Supper would be simple, cornbread and leftover stew, but there was butter and even honey for the bread.

As Mary placed tankards on the fine walnut table, voices came through the open doorway. The elder Russell, known to all as "Grandda," entered the kitchen. His spectacles reflected the light of hearth and lantern and hid his eyes, but his warm smile could not be disguised.

"I smell bacon." Grandda found a chair. "Agnes May, ye put bacon in everything."

"My receipts are my own to keep. But ye may guess."

Mr. May and Mr. MacLeod entered and took their places at the table.

Mary fetched the children and waited for the prayer. With John Russell away, his father took over the duties of family worship. After supper they'd listen to a reading of Scripture and a bit from a book.

Arch May buttered a chunk of steaming cornbread. "Grandda, what's the reading tonight?"

"Genesis 34. Then we start *Julius Caesar*. Shakespeare."

Iain MacLeod raised a brow. "Sounds lively."

Mary wiped Tommy's face and released him to sit on the floor. Russell's Ridge was a warm place. She wouldn't be here forever. But one thing she'd do while here—learn all she could, prepare all she could, for the future.

She rose and took the dishes to the sudsy bucket to soak. Tomorrow she'd ask Mrs. May the way of the madder plant. Perhaps she could grow it herself.

Agnes May sold the madder to a shop in Richmond. She could do the same.

And never need a man again.

* * *

IAIN ENTERED the barn and sought out the mare in her stall. "Hey, Willow," he murmured.

The mare lifted her head and flared her nostrils.

Ian checked her water and gave her some hay but no grain. She nosed the offering but took only a single mouthful. He found a curry brush in the corner and gave her an unnecessary grooming.

She wasn't due to foal for at least another week, but the signs were all there. He'd brought her to the barn this morning, noticing the swollen udder. Now the teats glistened wet.

Well, then. He'd sleep here tonight.

After supper, he fetched a blanket and lantern from his lonely cabin, now finished but empty of all but the essentials he needed to eat and sleep, plus a few keepsakes. And the green Testament.

Back at the barn, he left the lantern and a fire starter box on a keg near the door, and arranged the blanket over some straw. He unbuckled his belt.

"Ho, Willow, g'night now." Ian closed his eyes, but sleep eluded him. John Russell was somewhere up north with that General Braddock, fighting alongside redcoats against the French—and the Indians.

Iain couldn't imagine fighting alongside redcoats. The

smoke over Culloden moor appeared behind his eyelids, MacDonald red flashing now and again.

He still couldn't remember the search for his fallen father, not really; the blow to his head had driven it away. Perhaps it was for the best, for what he did remember—the corbies circling, the shots fired in the distance—all of that had a nightmarish, ghoulish quality that he'd almost forgotten. Had tried to forget.

He could forgive the Campbells—almost. If he ever saw the laird face-to-face Iain would give him a right hook, for sure. A man could settle an honest dispute with an honest blow. But the Duke of Cumberland was another thing entirely.

The minister said even the rulers were subject to God. That God raised up rulers and set them down again.

But surely God didn't hold with the rape of Scotland. It was inconceivable. Did God see?

A new question popped into his mind—did God see him?

Straw poked through the blanket, and Iain turned restlessly.

What God did in the affairs of nations was one thing. But what about individuals? When the Russells prayed, they prayed as if God were right there in the room.

He tossed again, weary but unsettled.

The mare shifted once and quieted. Her presence soothed him, and finally, he slept.

* * *

IAIN WASN'T sure what woke him. It was still full dark. The mare was moving nervously, the straw in her stall snapping and shifting, and the donkey was braying in the distance like a tolling bell sounding the alarm.

Iain jumped up, got tangled in the blanket, and fell. He scrambled up again and grabbed the lantern.

A chorus of panicked bleating came from the sheepfold, a patchwork enclosure bordered on one side by a gnarly rhododendron thicket. Behind him, the mare whinnied in distress. She heard something—maybe smelled something.

Iain grabbed his belt and drew his long knife from its sheath, then opened the barn door. He wished for a musket.

What could it be? A wolf? A great cat? Painters hunted at dawn. The night felt old, the dark just before dawn, perfect time for a cat.

A screech and a tumult made him drop the lantern—he had no time to light it. He needed to save the sheep, no matter if he was blind.

He charged across the yard.

"Hey, scat!"

He blinked, realizing that while there was no moon, starlight cast ethereal patches on the ground between the trees just ahead. He wasn't totally blind.

A squeal, a feline growl, then silence.

Iain strode along the path to the sheepfold, reached for the nearest rail, and listened intently. The sheep inside were pressed against the far side, whining and bleating.

The cat was not here.

Where was the ram?

Feeling along he discovered a rail knocked from the fence. Had the ram, Samson, knocked it down? Ian would not be surprised. He took a deep breath, knife at the ready, unable to do more in the dark.

He heard only the occasional bleats and snorts of the sheep over the sound of his own breathing. Assuming it was a great cat, he couldn't charge it in the dark with only a knife. The ewes were safe behind him. He could wait.

The donkey stopped braying. A lone bird chirped. Tree trunks loomed as misty shapes around him. The predawn gray sent its tendrils through the woods.

The cat must be gone.

Carefully Iain examined the foliage. A broken twig, a cloven depression in the leaf mold. He followed the breakage, knife at the ready.

He didn't have far to go before the ram's stink washed over him. The broken body of Samson lay thirty feet from the fold.

Grief caught at his throat and stopped his breath. He glanced about, wary of the cat, but saw nothing. The ram's neck lay at an awkward angle, but there was little blood.

He knelt and stretched a hand to Samson's pelt. The stubborn creature was still warm. "Sorry, lad."

Is e Dia fhèin as buachaill dhomh, cha bhi mi ann an dìth ...

Shepherd. The Lord is my shepherd. The words of the psalm smote Ian with a cleansing force, like rain on a hot day.

Did God look on him as he looked on this rascally ram? Care for him—despite all?

Iain had heard this psalm from his childhood. Now it was real.

He looked up at the peaceful foliage and the pink sky beyond. He didn't know how it could be, only that it was— the Lord was *his* shepherd.

CHAPTER 15

*M*ary rose to her feet and gazed at the small plants with satisfaction, their glad leaves arranged in whorls on the stalks. Tiny swellings on one specimen alarmed her.

She pointed. "What's this?"

Agnes May took a step forward but did not attempt to squat. "Flower buds. In a few weeks, ye'll see wee white flowers—very bonny when ye've got a lot of plants."

Mrs. May did have a lot of madder—the plants spread by runners underground, and now Mary had the satisfaction of her own madder patch, on her own property. She glanced around. The area they had chosen had plenty of sun but was close enough to the stream to haul water. Plenty of room to spread.

"How long until harvest?"

"Let it grow, lass. You could start digging up the roots

after two years, but I'd give it three. If ye like, we could add a few more slips next spring. Either way, I dinna think ye need to fret about water. They're established now, no need to come back every week."

"Thank you—I cannot tell you how—"

"Hah! I havena done laundry for months now. This is nothing. Let's get on back, I need to mind the dinner."

They retrieved the mule and put him in harness. Mary could walk the short distance between Russell's Ridge and her property, but Mrs. May's knees pained her.

Clambering in the tiny cart, Mary took one more look behind her. The sale of madder root was one more way to feed her children. She missed Simon, but she refused to mourn over the fact that he was a poor provider.

Well, a woman could manage on her own.

The mule made easy work of the distance, but they hadn't quite reached the house when a man appeared on the path from the stream.

Red hair—it was Roy Russell, or "Uncle Roy," as the children called him. Every line in his body was tight, tense. He spotted them. "Ladies," he said, hat in hand. "Where's Grandda? Arch?"

Fear clutched at Mary. "Has something happened?" The men were up north fighting. There had been rumors of a terrible defeat in the north, but no reliable news yet.

He studied them, opened his mouth as if to speak, then closed it. "Auntie Agnes, would ye let your husband know we've had word?"

Roy went to fetch Iain MacLeod while Mary knocked as firmly as she dared on the door of the nearby cabin. Grandda emerged, and soon the residents of the Ridge were gathered around the walnut table in the kitchen of the big house. Mary served ale and cider with trembling hands.

Roy Russell motioned her to sit. "I've terrible news—not of our folks, but of the sheriff. He's been killed by Indians. Down south."

Mary's mouth fell open. Sheriff Patton was the most important magistrate of Augusta County. She'd seen him several times at the meetinghouse—a tall, intimidating man. She couldn't imagine him dead.

Simon might be glad. Simon hated him.

Arch May clamped his hands around his tankard. "How?" The question emerged almost as a statement.

"Patton brought over settlers for a tract he owns down south. He was visiting there with his nephew—"

"William!" Mrs. May's eyes rounded with concern.

Mary's heart leaped. William Preston was kind, with a smile for everyone.

"Young Preston is safe. He was off on an errand when the Shawnee fell upon the settlement."

A line appeared between Iain MacLeod's brows. "But why there? The French are up north."

Everyone looked at Iain.

She knew he'd spent time serving an Indian trader, traveling out west. If anyone understood the Indians, it was Iain. But even he didn't understand this.

Had the Shawnee declared war on the valley?

And why?

* * *

MARY ADDED a long chunk of oak to the crackling fire under the black wash kettle. She fetched the laundry and the soap while the fire matured and heated the water.

She dumped in the clothes—soiled linsey shirts, small

clothes, neckerchiefs, and aprons—to the steaming water and scooped out some of Abigail Russell's soft lye soap.

Mary grabbed the paddle and glanced up at the trees surrounding the Russells' home. She couldn't help herself, despite what Arch May had said, that the sheriff was killed many miles away. That the Shawnee wouldn't attack here.

No, he hadn't said they wouldn't attack here. Only that Sheriff Patton was killed over a hundred miles away.

A very long way. Did Indians have horses?

The trees remained still and peaceful, their shade a cool respite on a July morning.

Mary agitated the clothing in the soapy, steaming water. The effort calmed her. It was a solace to work alone like this, the children at the Mays' home, coaxed there on the pretext that Mrs. May needed help feeding the chickens. They would probably return streaked with dirt, their mouths red with jam.

She transferred the clothes to the rinse kettle. One of the shirts bobbed to the top. One of Ian MacLeod's, most probably. Arch May's shirts were hard to get completely clean. They were always streaked with soil from the fields and stained with things she couldn't identify. Ian's clothes smelled of horses and sweat but were never filthy.

Mary thrust the floating shirt below the surface, forcing her thoughts away from Ian MacLeod or what his clothes smelled like. She was married and had no right to think about those things.

It was noon before she finished hanging up the clothes. A sudden breeze stirred the damp linen as she clipped on the last apron. Her shoulders ached and sweat gathered at her neckline. She'd wash the sheets tomorrow.

Voices—children's voices—piped high and clear up the narrow path to the Mays' cabin. Tommy appeared first, then Mrs. May, holding Joanie's hand. Hardly a babe anymore.

"Ho, Mary lass. I do think we'll get rain."

Mary looked at the darkening sky. "My wash—"

"Leave it, 'twill be fine."

The breeze freshened and fat drops fell on her face. "Come, Tommy, let's go inside." Distant hoofbeats beat a tattoo. Mary picked up Joanie and peered down the path. A rider was approaching—one of the Kerr lads.

"He's got news." Mrs. May's voice was tight.

The rider slowed his chestnut gelding as he neared them. Sweat tracked his dusty face.

"Ho, ladies, a letter from Mr. Russell."

That was good news. A letter meant John Russell was alive.

But what about Simon? He'd never bothered to write.

* * *

SEVERAL NEIGHBORS JOINED them as they entered the house. Mary herded the children in an empty corner. Lizzie and Roy had four, including the oldest, Ritchie, who sat with the men.

Roy Russell opened the letter, hovering next to the walnut table while the others found seats on chairs, stools, or on the floor. "Jamie was injured, but he should recover."

"Sit and read," Mrs. May chided.

Mary poured ale into cups and tankards, her fingers flying. But she could not stop her hands from trembling. Was Simon safe? Would John Russell know?

Roy tugged off his neckerchief and wiped his forehead, then sat. He grabbed the tankard in front of him and drank, his Adam's apple bobbing.

He opened the rumpled letter and began to read.

Will's Creek

15 July 1755

Dear Family and Friends at Russell's Ridge,

I have written separately to my wife in Richmond but knew you would wish the news.

I am well save for a few scratches, which James Paxton ably treated. As for the lad, he served bravely, and his injuries, while more serious than my own, are healing. Colonel Washington graciously invited him to his home on the Potomack River to recuperate.

General Braddock suffered a grave defeat. I shall not blame him, as he was a brave man and a fair general, by all accounts, but he did not know the country, nor the Indians. Washington kent better, of course, but the common soldiers jeered at him. Our progress was slow through the wilderness, and all was turmoil when the French attacked ten miles from Fort Duquesne. The militia were hampered as they wished to fight from the woods, but the regulars insisted on formal tactics.

No one told the Indians about formal tactics. They fought according to their own lights, hiding behind trees and falling upon the line of soldiers strung out along the path, vulnerable as sheep in a pen.

"Eejit!" Arch May broke in. "*I* blame the Sassenach general! Eejit!"

There were various murmurs of agreement. Mary listened quietly from her stool near the children. The French fort seemed far away, unimportant, but the mention of Indians sent chills down her back.

Roy waited until the comments subsided.

I am sorry to say a stray musket ball felled poor Cricket. A queen among horses, she served ably up to the last, not losing her head under fire. Neither did Red, the gelding Jamie rode. He gave the horse to Washington after the latter lost his own mount. The colonel lost several, I believe, and sustained a number of bullet holes through his coat. When night fell, there was no moon, but Washington bravely led us to safety.

I am thankful, for the Lord was gracious to me and mine, but the valley has lost a number of militiamen, including Simon McKee. I ask that you inform his widow in my stead.

Yours, John Russell

Mary sat frozen on her seat. Her pulse thudded in her ears, and her vision swirled.

"Good riddance," someone said—was it Ritchie?

"Shush, lad."

A warm arm slipped around Mary's back. "My poor lass." Mrs. May murmured, her breath warm with the smell of onions and ale. "My poor lass."

Mary sensed the room emptying. Whimpering, Joanie grabbed her skirts and pulled herself up on wobbly legs.

"Ma?" Tommy's voice. "Ma?"

There was no way to explain Simon's death to her children.

Not when she scarce believed it herself. But the yawning pit in her soul was real enough.

"No shame in weeping," Mrs. May said. "No shame a t'all."

The room swam behind her tears.

CHAPTER 16

*M*ary added a small amount of turpentine to the warm beeswax mixture and stirred. It would thicken as it cooled, but she meant to use it straightway, nice and workable.

She scooped out a small amount of the polish and plopped it onto the clean walnut table. With a rag she spread it vigorously over the surface of the wood, the tang of the turpentine sharp in her nose.

The house was empty for once, and the ache in her chest reminded her that she was truly alone.

A widow.

Three weeks now, and she still grappled to believe it.

Mary refocused on the task. The walnut was beautiful, only needing a bit of attention to bring out the beauty of the grain. Even back at the Byrds' plantation, polishing furniture had been a favorite task. How much more here at Russell's Ridge, where there was no fear of trouble, only the cheerful voice of a mockingbird through the open door.

Yes, she was alone.

Perhaps it was for the best.

She lent her weight to her strokes, feeling guilty for thinking such a thing. How could she possibly be glad for Simon's death? She blinked away tears. It was confusing.

Exchanging the rag for a dry one, she returned to the table and ran the cloth over the wood again and again until her shoulders ached.

Mary stepped back. The table gleamed in the soft morning light, but the sight failed to cheer her.

Her gaze fell on a bit of white paper peeping out from under a heavy crock on a kitchen shelf. Abigail Russell's letter, where Mrs. May had stashed it.

The family was returning. What did that mean for her?

Would they send her back home? They truly didn't need a housekeeper. Mary suspected she didn't clean as well as the gentle but fastidious matriarch of the family.

Maybe she should go home. Swallows were nesting in the eaves of the humble cabin, and the inside was worse. Mouse droppings and cobwebs.

She could clean all that in a single day. There was plenty of time to gather chestnuts.

But there was no crop in the field, no meat hanging in a smokehouse, nothing in the tiny pantry. They'd starve if they went back this year.

She reached for the Windsor chair. Her fingers polished each finely lathed spindle with movements easy with practice. No, her children needed to eat. She'd stay.

Iain's fresh-smelling cabin flashed in her mind's eye. She'd helped Mrs. May hang curtains when the chinking was done.

She huffed a private rebuke. No need to be thinking of him. And she redoubled her resolve not to rely on a man... ever again.

* * *

IAIN CRADLED the hand-carved crook in his arms as he sat watching the sheep. The September sun felt warm on his neck, and the croon of insects and birds lulled him, but every few minutes, he scanned the tree line for trouble.

He wasn't really worried. The donkey grazing behind him had as good a nose as any dog. Before him the grazing sheep drifted like fluffy white ships over the pasture, three months' growth of fleece sufficiently thick that the bell that the bell-wether wore was barely visible.

Iain plucked a stem from the grass and chewed it thoughtfully. The Kerr lads had helped with the shearing. He smiled at the memory of their clumsiness, but they'd been given a large fleece for their efforts.

He scanned the flock. Six mature ewes, three yearlings, and a handful of likely lambs. The sight of the lambswool had made Mrs. May smile. She had a table loom now. All of it was John Russell's doing.

The man was an indefatigable worker. And a generous man, forbye. When Ian's contract had been fulfilled, Russell had offered him a heifer as payment for the next half year's labor. Iain had asked for sheep instead.

A slow smile had spread across Russell's face. "I am verily tired of sheep, myself. Take them, take them all, and all I ask is half the fleeces. The ones born under your care are yours free and clear."

But without a ram, there would be no new lambs. A problem that hopefully would not last long. Robinson should return from Triple Forks soon.

Iain's glance wandered to the line of cottonwoods to the north. Mrs. McKee's land. Her grief was difficult to watch.

Guilt rose up in him again. He'd wished the man dead—

but the reality was a sore trial. How a woman could grieve the loss of such a man he did not quite understand. Maybe she'd loved him—or loved him once.

Iain wished he could comfort her somehow. But she had constructed fences around herself—strong fences—and she barely spoke to him. At least she had Mrs. May, and now Mrs. Russell, since she'd returned.

Motion caught his eye. Something—or someone—was moving on the path along the river. First the bobbing head of a mule appeared, then a thatch of brown hair. It was Robinson driving his wagon.

Sally, the mule, emerged fully into view, a tough but patient creature. She pulled the wagon and plowed the fields, and she tolerated the attentions of Robinson's flock of children, who seemed to imagine the animal was a toy. No normal self-respecting mule would put up with it, but Sally did.

"Howdy." Robinson raised his hand in greeting and drew the mule to a stop, whereupon she bent her head and snuffed the grass at the side of the path.

The donkey brayed a noisy greeting, and the mule swung an ear in his direction but was otherwise unimpressed.

Robinson jumped off the wagon seat, and Iain scanned the bed of the wagon. A moppy white head looked around curiously. The yearling ram he'd been hoping for.

"What have ye for me?" Iain had asked Robinson to take an animal to market. A straight-up trade, yearling for yearling, had been the plan.

Robinson grinned. "Old McCullough north of Triple Forks has Leicesters. Claims they're something special." He searched Ian's face. "Aren't they?"

Robinson knew nothing of sheep.

"I've heard of them. Show me."

The man loosed the animal and set it down where it wobbled unsteadily for a moment. It was small and spindly for a yearling. And its face was speckled. But the fleece looked interesting.

"He's small."

"As for that… he's not a yearling."

"Spring lamb?" In that case, the creature would be large and sturdy full-grown. He approached the animal slowly and took the end of the rope from Robinson's hands. Iain fingered the fleece. The wool was long, the texture silky. "What did you say he was?"

"Leicester. Will it do?" Robinson's forehead sprouted worry lines.

"Well done, I'd say."

"McCullough said he'd discount him on account of all the spots. He threw in a suckling pig and something else."

Iain smiled, envisioning the dickering. But he couldn't have done a better job if he'd been there. The Leicester would improve the entire flock.

Robinson went back to the wagon. Over his shoulder he asked, "The missus back safe? And Miss Susanna?" He produced a wiggling sack. He placed it on his shoulder like a woman burping a babe.

"Miss Russell's still in Williamsburg."

"Miss Susanna might marry a posh Randolph if she stays much longer. That'll be a disappointment to young Paxton. Can you use a pig? It's a runt." A snout protruded from the mouth of the sack.

Mary McKee had said once that she wanted pigs. Hogs were the easiest livestock to mind after chickens. Every autumn they fattened themselves on fallen nuts in the woods, and during the crisp weather of December, hogs were butchered all over the valley.

"Oh aye, a pig is welcome."

Robinson passed him the squirming sack and glanced at the cottonwoods. "The widow McKee gone home?"

The man was worse than a gossiping woman. "Nay, I hear she'll stay the winter."

Robinson harrumphed a reply and rummaged in his pocket. "Old man McCullough liked your animal. Threw in this."

He opened his hand. It was a Scottish clasp, a pin featuring a traditional thistle design. Meant for a kilt or a cloak.

A cloak. "That's verra nice. Ye did a canny trade, Robinson." He might not be able to get through the widow's fences, but he could at least bless her in small ways.

* * *

MARY HUMMED to herself as she reached for the pins holding the sheet to the line. Mrs. Russell's presence was a comfort, and the children cheered her. Nathan and Hannah played with her bairns and helped keep them out of trouble.

And apparently, no one wanted to do the laundry. Which was understandable. Mrs. Russell made fine soap; even her ordinary gray laundry soap was gentler than most, and the special batches she made for bathing were scented with herbs. Even so, laundry was hard work. And Mrs. Russell was clearly expecting another child.

Mary didn't mind. Laundry and mending were tasks she did well. She knew how to spin. Week by week she was learning more about dyeing and weaving. So, when Mrs. Russell invited her to stay on, she had plenty of reason.

Mrs. May had a table loom Mr. Russell had made her

from a pattern he'd gotten somewhere, and already she'd made a beautiful shawl from Russell wool.

"Granted," Mrs. May had explained, "'tis not a proper loom like Mr. Kerr's, but I can sew three or four of these together to make a blanket."

Mary resolved to learn the way of the loom as well. Shawls and blankets she could sell. Besides, she was beginning to love Mrs. May as a mother. Staying here would enable her to help in small ways. And it would keep away the brooding shadow of grief.

In three deft motions, the fresh-smelling sheet was folded and settled in the basket. She moved on to the next. In two minutes, all the linens tucked away. She picked up the basket and walked to the house.

No sooner was she inside when she heard a halloo.

Iain MacLeod was coming up the path, carrying a sack. Strangely, the sack wriggled.

"Mr. Russell's out to the barn," she said. Surely Ian was looking for him.

But Iain's clear blue gaze was fixed on her as he came up to the doorway. "Ma'am." He reached for his hat in a formal gesture—why he wanted to tip his hat to her she did not know—and she took a half step back.

The sack on his shoulder opened slightly to reveal a hoggish snout. And in that moment the creature redoubled its struggles.

It flew at her and landed in the basket. Startled, she dropped it.

A flurry of snout and legs resolved into a young pig, which promptly ran about the kitchen, its tiny hooves skittering over the floor.

Mrs. Russell entered the room, her mouth an O.

"I'm sorry..." Iain's voice was swallowed up in the commotion.

"Mr. MacLeod," Mrs. Russell said, "we need a crate."

He left, and Mrs. Russell darted to the kitchen shelves and reached for the buttermilk crock. She poured a small dish full of the thin milk.

Mary squatted at the door to prevent the pig from escaping, and Mrs. Russell set the dish down. She crumbled a bit of yesterday's cornbread into it.

The pig's wild motions slowed, and it cocked its ears toward the dish. Ian entered with the crate, set it sideways, and scooted the dish inside.

"She'll get used to eating here," Iain instructed. "Put some sacking in there. Then in a few days you can move her outside. She'll know where her food is."

Mary stared at the creature, now nosing the dish. *She?* A sow was good news. In a year she'd have more. The Russells owned a sow and a boar, which had wasted no time in producing offspring.

The little pig was clearly a gift. But Mr. Byrd had given gifts. And Simon. "My laundry!" She stood and eyed Iain. "Thank you kindly. But I'll need to wash the sheets again."

Iain paused only a moment before he spoke. "I'll do it. Just give me the soap."

Mary's knees seemed to weaken and she sat on the nearest chair. She had no defense against kindness.

* * *

IAIN OPENED the green Testament in the fading light. The evening shadows arrived sooner now in the last crisp month of autumn, and he attempted to read the Scriptures before supper, not after, when the light of hearth and candle flickered across the page, rendering the small type difficult to decipher.

Accepted in the Beloved ... adopted ...

Ephesians was puzzling. But it no longer unsettled him. Here and there bright glimpses of God's lovingkindness— His *tròcair*—warmed Iain's heart.

Accepted ... adopted ...

A sharp rap at the door was followed by the door opening.

"Reading?" Agnes May shut the door behind her, but not before a chill draft swirled against Ian's ankles. "I've brought you something."

She carried a large white lump. Ian opened his mouth to ask her what it was.

"A pillow," she explained, before he could say anything. Her gaze swept over the single large room that served as parlor, kitchen, and bedroom. The pallet he slept on was now positioned in the middle of the floor so he would benefit from the heat of the hearth. She stared at it. "Is that all ye have for a bed?"

"Aye." Iain had slept on much worse. "Ye helped me with it at the time."

"So I did. But 'tis no bed, no' a proper one." She placed the pillow at the head of the pallet.

"I dinna need more."

She cut him a curious glance. "And so what happens if ye marry?" Her raised brow told him all she had to say about that.

Leave it to a woman to point out. "Well…"

"I need ye to go hunting with Arch tomorrow. I asked him for ducks."

Iain nodded. "The Kerr lads can manage the sheep. Geese?"

"Mark where they are—I'll want several for Christmas."

He closed the Testament. The way Mrs. May was eyeing his bed, he knew she had designs on the feathers.

Well, he'd not gainsay the plans of such a woman.

The cabin was too big for one.

But Mary didn't want the attentions of a man.

CHAPTER 17

MARCH 1756

*I*ain swung the axe through its arc and the chunk of oak split satisfyingly in two.

"Mister Ian, come!" Seven-year-old Tommy McKee bounced up the path. "Miss Susanna is here! And there's cake!"

Joanie ran up beside her brother. "Cake!" she echoed.

The children were growing so quickly. Over the winter, Joanie had collected new words like a magpie.

Iain set the axe down on the chopping block. He was sweaty despite the cool spring breeze. "I'll be yonder presently. Does Mrs. May need wood?"

The woodbox at the house was full, he was sure, but the children liked to feel important. He handed each child a piece of kindling to bring back. Then he went inside his cabin, splashed his head and neck from the basin, and rubbed himself dry with a towel. He pulled on a fresh shirt for the celebration.

He'd spotted the arrival of the horses and wagon from his property an hour ago, but felt hesitant to rush to greet the family. Susanna had joined them in Richmond, and they'd just now returned. John Russell had brought his daughter home.

Was she truly wayward, as some whispered? Was she now affianced to some fancy member of the first families of Virginia?

He re-tied his hair and set off for the house.

Roy Russell and his wife Lizzie stood at the open door. Ian hung back. Arch appeared carrying a plank, bellowing.

"Roy, grab the end!"

Together they set up a trestle table outside. Iain stepped into the shadows at the edge of the yard. Mrs. Russell brought out two flasks and set them on the table. Mary McKee began to pour drinks.

Hearty conversation floated over Russell's Ridge. Iain ventured to pick up a cup, watching Mary. She glanced at him only once. As if he were part of the background, like a tree or a bush. She went inside.

He sighed.

Laughter came from the house, and he glimpsed Susanna's dark hair through the doorway. Mrs. May came outside with cake. "The bairns have been fed, I've brought ye gents the leavings."

Young Jonathan Russell emerged from the house, crumbs on his lip. His gaze fell on Iain. "I drove the wagon over the Gap."

"The horses mind ye?"

The lad smiled. "Da says I'll make a horseman yet."

"And that ye will."

Jonathan darted off to rejoin the other lads. A mantle of loneliness fell over Iain. He drained his cup and slipped off into the darkness. The one he'd love to speak to didn't care for him at all.

Help, Lord. Help her. Help me.

* * *

IAIN SLIPPED into the barn before dawn. "Come now, bonnie lass," he crooned to the mare Percy. He led her to the paddock and returned to muck out the stall. Most of the horses stayed in the paddock overnight; only a few—older animals or those about to foal—were given space in the modest barn.

He grabbed the pitchfork under the watchful gaze of a new equine face. Susanna's mare. He couldn't think of the name. A Connemara pony.

The gray light of dawn filtered in as he replaced the straw.

"G'd morning." Susanna stood at the entrance.

"Howdy." Iain wiped straw off his face.

Susanna crossed to the pony and stroked her face. "I didn't see you last night."

"I had some cake."

She led the mare out to the paddock and returned.

Iain still clutched the pitchfork. "I'll clean the stall."

"Thank you."

"Rumor has it ye might be wed to some fancy gent in Williamsburg."

Susanna chuckled, but it wasn't entirely a mirthful sound. "There are certainly a lot of embroidered waistcoats there, to be sure." She laid her head on the pony's stall door and heaved a sigh of contentment. "I am happy to be home."

"Will Mr. Paxton return soon? I heard he recovered from his injuries in the war."

Susanna seemed to fight a grin. "I saw him in Hanover County. He's a minister now." She shrugged. "I do not know where he will go next. I do not think he knows."

Ian knew little of ministers and their calling. So he simply grunted in response.

She slipped out, and Iain cleaned the stall. He opened the paddock gate and released the horses into the pasture, then turned and strode toward the house. His stomach rumbled. Breakfast would be ready.

John Russell met him before the door. "Now that my daughter is back, I want to practice getting to the cavern." He went over the details.

Like white men, the Shawnee would go to war in warm weather. And unlike white men, there was never any warning.

Iain went about his labors with half an ear listening for the signal. After the noon meal he started to relax. He was with the sheep on his property when a shot rang out.

The donkey brayed at the sound. Iain hesitated only half a second, then darted toward the Mays' cabin. Then he redirected his path to the cavern. The Mays lived close to the hideout; he'd go there first.

Mary—where would she be?

He arrived, panting, at the chestnut tree, just in time to see Susanna's dark head disappear below. Arch was helping John Russell supervise. Ian didn't see Mrs. May—perhaps she was already below.

Mary scurried up. "I can't find Tommy."

"Never mind," Iain said. "I'll fetch him."

The lad was likely at the spring—or the stream. He loved to splash in the shallows or catch minnows.

It was only practice. But what if the attack were real? Iain sped toward the spring. No luck. He ran to the stream, scooped up Tommy, and placed him on his shoulder for the trip back.

"Uncle Iain! Put me down!"

"Nay, lad." Ian gasped for air. "Hear the shot?"

"Oh."

When he returned, only John Russell remained above ground. Worry lines marked his forehead.

They'd taken too long.

MARY MARVELED at the sight of the madder on her property. The plants were taking over the clearing. *Next year.* Next year she'd dig up a few of the roots, use them herself for dyeing. And the year after that, she'd have a crop large enough to sell.

She returned to the Ridge, cutting across Iain MacLeod's property. The sheep browsed the summer growth, their heads facing all the same way. One of them raised his head and stared at her—the new ram, clearly cognizant of his duty even at such a young age.

She passed through the Mays' orchard. Ahead the big house came into view. Nearby, a horse she didn't recognize was tied up—a dusty, sweaty horse.

A visitor. She slowed. Before she reached the house, a man came out, mounted the horse, and departed. Daisy barked once at the rider, then sat, letting her tongue run out.

A messenger? And if so, what kind of news had he brought?

She quickened her steps, and by the time she entered the

house, the family was in turmoil. A crease between her brows, Mrs. Russell was packing a basket.

Susanna looked pale. She splashed water on her face and dried it with a kitchen towel before spotting Mary.

"Neighbors' baby is coming."

Mrs. Russell looked up. "Mary, would you help Agnes with supper? I must go."

"Of course." Something was wrong.

They left, and Mary followed to the door. Was the baby going to be a difficult birth?

Or was it a difficult situation, like her own first babe?

Outside, John Russell was speaking with Iain and Arch May near the chopping block. She could not hear their words, but their faces were grim.

Even the dog seemed subdued.

Mary turned back into the house. Several tankards sat abandoned on the table, one half full. She picked up the empty ones and proceeded to wash them, her mind spinning.

Was it the babe? Or something else?

Could it be the Shawnee? A chill ran down her spine.

She set the cleaned and dried tankards upside down on the kitchen shelf and wandered back to the doorway, where she almost collided with Iain MacLeod. The other men were gone.

"Mary."

He never called her that—always "Mrs. McKee."

"What has happened?"

His mouth opened and closed before he finally spoke. "Come sit."

"I'm not delicate."

He said nothing but picked up the lone tankard and set it down again. "Indians. George Painter's farm. A number killed… many captured." He sat down at the table and continued to stare at the vessel.

"Where?" Weak at the knees, Mary grabbed a stool and sat. He wasn't telling her everything.

He met her gaze. "It's down valley a day's journey or so. Toward Winchester."

The geography of the Shenandoah Valley was still vague in her mind. "Up north."

"Aye." Ian rubbed his stubbly cheek.

"The last big raid was down south. This one is north of us—"

"But we are more than twenty miles east of Buffalo Gap. Any Shawnee would have to cross the valley to get here."

She studied his face. Iain MacLeod knew Indians. "How much difference does that make to them?"

He looked away. "Not much."

Her children. At least there was a place to hide, the cavern. If they could reach it quickly enough.

* * *

THE SUMMER CREPT INTERMINABLY BY. Mary washed laundry, taught Tommy his letters with Mrs. Russell's primer, and mended several shirts, the exertion of barley harvest and hay cutting ripping holes and loosening seams.

Some mornings Mrs. May brought the loom to the kitchen table, and Susanna helped her. But this morning, Mary took Susanna's place, as the lass had gone out hunting ginseng.

"Come. This piece"—Mrs. May pointed—"is called the heddle."

Indigo blue yarn was threaded through narrow slots in a piece of wood—the heddle—and wrapped around a fat peg on the far side of the table. A large skein of undyed yarn sat nearby, presumably for the shuttle.

Mary had glimpsed the procedure—threading the heddle took a fair amount of time. "I'll prepare the shuttle."

They worked silently, the peaceful morning filled with the gentle sounds of children playing outside. The project was a third finished when they had to stop, but not before the color was revealed, a soft heather blue.

Mrs. May set the loom aside. "Ye think Iain'll like it?"

Mary's cheeks warmed.

Mrs. May grinned. "Ye canna weave a kilt on this, but it makes fine scarves. Men dinna like bright colors, unless it's a kilt, of course." She strode to the door. "Can ye finish the stew? I need to see to the turnips in my kailyard."

Normally Mary assisted Mrs. May in the garden, but clearly, she wasn't wanted.

Mrs. May left, and Mary peeked out the door to see Daisy trailing the other woman. Where were the children? Their happy noises had vanished.

Fear pricked at her.

The stream—Tommy might be at the stream.

* * *

IAIN WOKE BEFORE DAWN, the snort of the cow in his ears. As he moved, the straw dust of the barn tickled his nose.

He sneezed. A horse shifted in a nearby stall.

"Morning, Charcoal." Susanna's pony was in the pasture, but he'd brought Charcoal inside for the night. He was training the black three-year-old to saddle and wanted to spend more time with him.

And he'd been sleeping here for the last several nights. His cabin was simply too far from the house, and Indians could attack at any time of day. He'd sneaked past the Mays' property with his blankets tucked up under his arm and created a bed over some straw. He wasn't fussy, though Agnes May would scold him if she found out.

Standing, he fastened his belt, heavy with the weight of his knife in its sheath. Sleeping in the barn was not much different than sleeping on the pallet in his cabin—especially at this time of year. He didn't need a fire, and he didn't need Agnes May's pillow.

He felt for his tomahawk where he'd left it against the wall. He picked it up and ran his hands over the smooth wood. Then he tucked it in his belt. Arch May owned a Scottish claymore, a heavy two-handed sword much like his own father's. Iain had no firearm or sword. But he could fashion a targe out of the top of a whiskey barrel. Hides would make it impervious to arrows.

It was a plan. But he still felt helpless. Strangely, he didn't fear death for himself, but his heart yearned over the lives of the women and children. At Woodstock, the Shawnee had not spared the young. He hadn't given Mary any details. No need.

After morning chores, he ate a quick breakfast, then returned to the barn.

He led Charcoal out. The youngest of Cricket's colts, the animal was lively but not mean. He was just young and healthy.

"See this?" Iain held up a saddle blanket to Charcoal's nose. "Not a danger. No problem at all."

The colt flared his nostrils and jerked his head.

He crooned to the horse, babbling nonsense as he wiped the animal's neck and side with the blanket. "Nae danger, none a t'all. Braw laddie, what a good fellow ye are."

He slipped the blanket over the colt's back. The horse hopped once, but his ears stayed forward. He wasn't alarmed.

Ian slipped off the blanket and led him back to the barn. "I'll put something interesting in the trough for you. Such a canny creature ye are."

The Shawnee would love such an animal. A thought struck him. He'd keep Charcoal in the clearing for the next month, feed the colt hay and corn to supplement the sparse grass, and continue to train him. Indians often traveled west in the fall, looking for good hunting. They built up stores of venison and buffalo in their winter camps and wouldn't travel east after harvest. After the corn was shucked, Russell's Ridge would be safe.

But if they came before then, the horse would be here, near the house, a distraction. And capturing and managing such a beast would take up energies they wouldn't have left for killing.

He tied Charcoal to a sapling, then mucked out the barn.

When he was finished, he wiped his face. It was hot already and not even noon. He forked some hay before Charcoal and sprinkled some corn over it.

The donkey brayed in the distance.

Ian turned toward the sound, fear snaking down his spine.

Daisy barked twice, but the sound was far away, toward the Mays' home. She must have followed Mrs. May up there.

Charcoal tossed his head.

The dog barked again and kept barking, a continuous, furious sound.

Ian pulled the halter off the animal's head, releasing him.

Arch May bellowed from beyond the trees.

CHAPTER 18

$\mathcal{M}$ary found Tommy at the stream, mud to his elbows. "Come to the house—no wait. Wash first."

A blue jay screamed somewhere, and the Mays' donkey brayed in the distance, like an alarm bell.

She squatted and helped her son. Daisy barked once, a faint sound. The dog must still be at the Mays'.

But what was she barking at?

Mary straightened and stood listening. Just when she thought she had imagined the sound, the dog barked again, and kept barking.

"Come, Tommy." Her voice emerged tight and high.

A man's shout—it was Arch May, she was sure.

Panicking, she grabbed Tommy, hoisted him to her shoulder, and trotted in the direction of the cavern. Joanie—where was Joanie?

"Ma, let me down!"

He seemed to gain weight with each step. Halfway there, she let him down, grabbed his hand, and they ran together.

A shot rang out, the sound coming from the direction of the Mays' home.

Mary arrived at the chestnut tree out of breath. John Russell crouched at the entrance to the cavern, passing Hannah to strong hands below. He stood, turned, and handed Tommy down.

She turned. "I need to get Joanie—"

"Nay. I'll go."

She hesitated. But Russell urged her, and she picked up her skirts and went below, every step wrenching at her heart.

Joanie!

Oh God, protect her! Save her!

* * *

IAIN'S HEART leaped at the sound of Arch's voice. He looked around the clearing in front of the house and barn, but he saw no one. Where were the children?

Where was Mary?

He dashed to the spring. The springhouse sat silent, the cold pool around it undisturbed.

A shot rang out in the distance.

Heart hammering, he dashed back. But only Charcoal remained in the clearing, dancing nervously.

Iain passed the barn and approached the house. Was no one inside? Surely, they'd have investigated the ruckus by now.

A child's cry alerted him. Joanie was standing in the doorway with a blanket, looking like she'd just woken up.

He ran. The Indians would be upon them at any moment. Just as he snatched her up, he caught a glimpse of red through the trees.

Shawnee? No, it was Susanna, back from foraging. Surely,

she'd heard the musket fire, she'd know to join him. He couldn't stop now.

He sped on, but out of the corner of his eye he saw her enter the clearing.

She was running toward the spring, her red skirt like a flag.

Running in the wrong direction.

No! Should he return? Why? Why would she run that way?

He had a suspicion, but his heart ached at the thought. He dodged low-hanging tree limbs and skidded to a stop. Russell was securing the cover of the cavern. He looked up at Iain's approach, saw the bairn, and dislodged the cover again. Iain handed Joanie to Russell, who passed her below.

Iain scanned the trees for a moment, listening. The dog had ceased barking. There was no glimpse of red, no evidence Susanna was coming. He slid down the rough-hewn steps and Russell closed them all up to darkness.

Just below Russell, Ian clung to the crudely hewn stone steps. He looked down. A single lantern cast a pale, trembling light on the faces below. Mary, Tommy, Joanie. Mrs. Russell, great with child, Jonathan at her side. Nathan crouched next to little Hannah, who was sucking her thumb.

"Where's Grandda?" Jonathan's plaintive voice.

"Shush," his mother said. "Grandda went to town with the Kerrs."

The Kerrs, the closest neighbors, would be safe. Roy and Lizzie had undoubtedly stayed to home, their house too far for a quick getaway. They might be safe at that distance, as long as the raiding party was not large and spread out.

The Mays—the Mays were not here. Iain's heart sank at the memory of Arch's bellow.

Oh Lord, help...

Above him, John Russell lifted the hide-out's cover an inch and peered out.

A faint whinny came to Iain's ears. *Charcoal.* Were they after the colt?

Silence fell, both inside and out.

Then Russell groaned softly, a moan he might not have known he made. "Susanna." The whisper was faint, a mere breath.

They waited so long Ian's hands began to stiffen on the stone. But in reality, it couldn't have been more than ten minutes.

Russell laid a hand on his shoulder. "I'm going out. Keep watch, I'll return shortly." He hesitated. "If something happens, stay here, dinna come after me."

Iain understood. John Russell might sacrifice himself, but Ian needed to stay back and protect the women and children.

Iain took his place at the top of the steps. Joanie whimpered below, and Mary shushed her.

There was little to see through the opening. He listened intently but heard only the occasional chirp of birds. A peaceful sound. Were the Indians gone?

Susanna. His suspicion grew. She must have seen Joanie in his arms and made a decision to distract the Shawnee, lure them away from the cavern, away from everyone.

Was she dead? Knowing the Shawnee, they'd probably capture her. But the Mays were old. Dread chilled his belly.

In less than a quarter hour Russell was back. "No sign of them." He instructed the rest to wait while he and Iain looked about.

Iain scrambled out of the hole and took a deep breath. What would they find? Russell wasn't saying. It couldn't be good.

They went to the house. The sight of Agnes May—alive—

brought tears to Iain's eyes. She was standing near the gnarly walnut tree on the path to the spring, clutching a musket and staring at something on the ground.

Russell placed a careful arm around the woman's shoulders. Iain drew near and followed her gaze—a foraging basket, but very little was inside. He read the tale: it had been dropped in a violent way, the contents scattered. A digging tool lay on the grass. Only one heavy ginseng root remained in the basket.

Susanna was alive. There was no other way to interpret this. There was no blood, no other evidence of trouble.

Where was Charcoal? Iain circled and studied the ground. The colt had left prints all the way to the spring. But there was no sign of him. Either the Indians had taken him or he'd run off.

But the question in the back of his mind returned: where was Arch May? If he wasn't with his wife—

Iain turned back to John Russell and watched him as he guided Mrs. May inside the house.

Then the man looked up, his eyes shiny with tears. "Fetch a horse. Get Mr. Craig and his wife."

The minister. Iain jogged to the pasture and chose the fastest animal. Now he knew what had happened.

Arch May was dead.

* * *

THE WAKE WAS PERFUNCTORY, without the usual gifts, with the exception of raisins and currants Mrs. Russell handed out to the children. Iain helped Roy Russell carry Arch's body on the board where it lay. They settled it on sawhorses in the Russell parlor.

A knitted watch cap nestled on Arch's head, strange in the

late summer warmth, concealing the man's butchered scalp. A clean shirt covered his other injuries.

He was still and pale, but it seemed that at any moment he'd open his eyes and make some joke or pithy comment. It was hard to believe he was gone.

Iain kept a steady, silent eye on Mrs. May as many of the prominent men of the area came and filed through the parlor.

Militia colonel Andrew Lewis laid his hand on Arch's cold brow. "A brave man. Curse the Injuns, they have no honor. Roy?"

Roy Russell looked up from across the room, where he sat with Grandda on a settle.

"I understand why John wished to track his daughter with only the Paxton lad. But it grates at me to stay behind," Lewis said.

Roy stood and placed his hands on his hips. "He fears the Shawnee will simply kill any captive slowing them down if they feel threatened by a large force."

Lewis sighed. "I understand. But what if—"

"Something happens to them?" Roy crossed his arms and looked at Iain. "What say you?"

"There's the matter of tracking them. Rain will wash away all evidence."

Lewis cleared his throat. "We know where they crossed Cowpasture Creek. I'll go today, get a sense of where they're headed."

"I'll join you," Robert Houston interrupted from the doorway. "I ken those parts."

The neighbors left the house with Roy and stood in a group, talking. Iain stayed inside with the elder Russell and the new widow, keeping vigil with the body. Mourners passed the bier silently, many touching the body in keeping with the old custom.

It was hard to believe that Arch May was dead. After losing everything in Scotland, Iain had gained a new family here.

Grief squeezed his insides. He'd lost his father all over again.

* * *

MARY WATCHED the minister as though from far away. The warm breeze toyed with Mr. Craig's forelock as he spoke at the head of the open grave. Mrs. Russell stayed close to Mrs. May at the minister's left, and Iain MacLeod looked into the sad trench from the other side.

Mary clutched her children's hands, feeling empty. The burial was sparsely attended, as if an Indian raid were a contagion. John Russell was gone, tracking the Shawnee with Jamie Paxton, and his absence was palpable.

Yesterday's horrors truly began when they all emerged from the cavern. Susanna was gone, a spilled basket marking the place of her capture. At least no blood colored the grass. She was alive, at least for now.

But Arch May was gone. Mrs. May stared into space, saying little at first. Mr. Russell kept them all away until Mrs. May emerged from her stupor and insisted that she needed to prepare his body and make his shroud.

Mary helped with the shroud. Agnes May took her sewing scissors and carefully snipped off a large square from Arch's new kilt, recently woven by the Kerrs. This she set aside. The rest of the fabric was doubled over. Mary sewed up one side, and as her needle found purchase for each stitch, her heart tore inside.

How could it be?

How could this happen? How could Arch May be dead?

The red hues of the fabric matched her swelling rage. She embraced it. Anger was better than succumbing to the torrent of grief that lapped at her mind.

When Mrs. May returned from washing her husband's body, she looked positively ancient, but her expression had cleared. The shock had eased.

She sat and took up her needle. "I'm sorry about Daisy. She were a fine, fechtie hound."

Mary didn't know what *fechtie* meant, but she could guess. The humble dog had courage. And now she was dead, buried at the edge of the Mays' cornfield, next to an Indian Arch had slain before succumbing to a rain of arrows. She could only imagine the scene. Arrows flying, Arch charging with his huge sword, the dog rushing the Indians, Agnes scrambling inside for the musket.

"If any of the biddies in town asks, tell them that dog is minding the Injun."

Mary's heart thawed a tiny bit at this glimpse of wry humor. Some of the people of the valley had strange ideas about the dead. But no matter her own confusion, she knew Arch May's soul was safe with God.

Her mind returned to the breezy Tinkling Springs grave-yard. Mr. Craig was quoting the Scriptures. "'O death, where is thy sting? O grave, where is thy victory?'"

He concluded with a prayer. Then Agnes bent down and picked up a clump of dirt. Mrs. Russell, her belly large with child, steadied her as she stepped to the edge of the grave and released her handful of soil.

The tiny thud on the casket seemed to echo in Mary's heart.

CHAPTER 19

*M*rs. Russell took the gleaming pistol from the high shelf near the door. "Just replace it here when you come in."

Mary still felt unsure about the loading process, but the main thing she needed to check was the priming, and she could manage that. "Where is the other one? Does Mrs. May have it?"

Mrs. Russell shook her head thoughtfully. "Nay, she says the musket is enough. Mr. MacLeod has the other."

Mary took a quick glance behind her. The children were all playing in the corner of the kitchen. Hannah and Joanie clucked over dolls, and Tommy sat quietly, lacing up a pair of moccasins. He'd wet the bed last night, the main evidence of the horrors they'd experienced just a few days before.

"I'll mind them," Mrs. Russell said. "I am getting too large for much else."

Mary estimated that only a month remained before the woman's confinement. Thankfully, the stress of the attack had not triggered early labor. "I'll fetch water and then see if there's any corn still green."

She reached for the pistol, checked the priming, and slid it into her pocket. Once out the door, she scanned the tree line. Her stomach tensed despite the peaceful chirping of a nuthatch that seemed to insist all was well. She scurried to the spring, the buckets knocking against her knees. Once the buckets were full, she walked back, forcing herself to take measured steps, braced by the weight of the water.

Mary examined the foliage behind the house one more time. Nothing was there. What was the chance that they'd be attacked again? She took a long, steadying breath. Fearful thoughts troubled her sleep, fear of what might happen, fear of what was happening to Susanna even now. The men hadn't returned.

She fought the fear. And she tried to pray for Susanna. But her prayers seemed useless. She wasn't worthy to approach God with the kind of certainty the Russells had.

She left the water inside, grabbed a basket for the corn, and soon she was striding down the path to the fields. On her left, partially dry stalks of corn filled the upper field. Across the way, the sheep nibbled at the remains of the barley, long since harvested. Trees belted the ends of the fields and flung out swaths of cool shade over the track.

A warm late-summer sun warmed her shoulders as she left the trees and gained a view of the river below, silver sparkles peeking from the trees along its bank. To her left the long sloping meadow had already been scalped for hay; to the right rail fencing marked out the lower cornfield, her destination.

Shouts startled her and she slowed, thrusting her hand into her pocket. Her fingers met the curved wood stock of the pistol.

"Shoo! Get!" Iain's voice.

Mary resumed breathing. It was only Iain. She resumed her pace and soon saw a commotion at the far end of the cornfield. Iain's head disappeared, then popped into view. He threw a rock, and a wild flapping of black wings rose like a cloud over the corn.

His gaze fell on her. She scanned the field. Most of the remaining green corn was near him. There was no help for it, she'd have to approach him.

She forced cheerfulness into her voice. "Blackbirds in the corn? I thought the Robinson lad was supposed to chase them off."

Iain squatted and picked up another rock. "Robinsons are shy of the Ridge just now. Dinna want their bairns near here."

Mary came closer, chose an ear, and wrestled it off the stalk. "I've an old sheet in the sewing basket."

Iain brightened. "Ye mean fashion a bird-scarer? I can bundle barley straw, attach bits of the sheet and maybe tin..."

Mary thrust another ear into the basket. Iain was easy to be with, as long as she guarded herself. She had seen the way he looked at her when he thought she wasn't looking. He had kind eyes. But he made her uncomfortable, too, because there was nothing in her that deserved that kind of affection.

He deserved someone better.

Iain turned abruptly, and Mary followed his gaze to see motion in the trees along the river. Her heart sped up, and she slid her hand into her pocket again.

"Charcoal—is that you, ye daftie lad!"

It was. The missing black colt meandered through the foliage and approached the grass on the verge of the road. He eyed Iain briefly, then settled in to graze unconcernedly.

Iain rubbed his jaw. "I'm that glad to see the creature. If

we approach him slowly, offer him some corn, he'll decide he wants to come home."

Mary trailed Iain, picturing what must have happened that day—an Indian following the elusive colt, never quite managing to catch him. She hadn't actually seen the raiding Indians, only imagined them as red specters with knives and tomahawks.

Iain turned and looked at her, concern in his eyes, as if he knew what she was thinking about. "How is Mrs. May this day?"

"She says 'nae Injun, nae devil will turn me out of my home.' She says she won't be ruled by fear."

He smiled grimly. "At least she's close by the house."

Mary's throat closed with sudden grief. Quietly they strolled toward Charcoal until they reached the colt, which extended his lips towards the corn in Ian's hand.

Iain scratched behind the horse's ears and patted his neck. "Good brawly lad."

Timidly, Mary stroked the colt's other side. With Ian here the size of the animal wasn't intimidating.

The horse shifted, his attention on the road. Mary followed the animal's gaze. Now she could hear it too: the soft clop-clop of hooves on dirt.

Soon riders appeared around a bend in the road. It was John Russell and Jamie Paxton, the lad studying to be a minister. Was Susanna with them? Mary's heart thudded in her chest. It seemed they'd been gone a long time, but it had only been a short span of days.

There was a third horse behind them. Was Susanna riding it?

Iain hallo'ed the men. Their tired faces told the tale. They hadn't rescued her. Jamie's eyes had dark circles under them, and he looked old, especially with his white hair. Folks said it was the war that had turned his hair white. He wasn't happy now.

Mary finally caught a good glimpse of the third rider—a stranger. She was sure she'd never seen him before. And yet, there was a vague familiarity about his features.

Russell reined in and dismounted. "We had to turn back," he said abruptly. Then his gaze fixed on Mary. "Fellow here says he's kin of yours."

"I have no kin." They were all dead now.

"Sam McKee," announced the stranger. "My brother owns land around these parts."

Mary shook her head. It couldn't be. Mrs. Borden had taken care of the land deeds for her, she was sure the land was hers—but she was just a woman.

"Now he's dead, I hear," the man said. She could see the resemblance. The dark hair, the scowl. "Now the land is mine."

Their faces began to spin. The whole world dimmed.

* * *

VOICES MURMURED ABOVE HER.

"Tomorrow, at the courthouse." John Russell's deep and comforting tones.

An answer, unintelligible, from a harsher voice.

Mary stirred and opened her eyes. She was supported by Iain's strong arm and the lumpy sedges along the fence line.

She sat up, still confused, just knowing that someone had threatened her.

"Ye fainted," Iain said.

Hoofbeats marked the location of the men as they rode up the path to the house.

"Where is—"

"McKee is gone. Dinna fash, we will see him tomorrow at the courthouse. The papers are all in order, I trust?"

The land—hers and Tommy's. "Yes. The courthouse has the originals. The Bordens made me copies."

She stood and swatted at her clothing. Her embarrassment was swallowed up in more important thoughts. "My husband mentioned a brother once, I'd forgotten."

Iain stood and looked about for Charcoal. The colt had edged away during the conversation. "He has no claim on the land, it was never Simon's. And even then—"

"He is a man." How could she make him understand?

Iain whistled to the colt and held out an ear of corn. "That makes no difference. Besides, Simon McKee was by no means popular here." He looked at her and his tone softened. "Ye ken that, aye? Folks knew... they knew he didn't provide well for his family. The Scripture says somewhat about that."

He glanced at her wrists and Mary remembered a day on the river when Iain must have seen bruising there. That's what he was really speaking of. Simon McKee was unpopular because folks suspected he beat his wife.

It was all very well and good to be sympathetic, but the reality was, Sam McKee was going to use some underhanded trick to steal her land. As a man, he had an advantage.

"I'm going," she said. "I'm going to the courthouse."

"There is no need—"

"Iain MacLeod, I am going. You can't understand. You're a man."

* * *

IAIN OBSERVED John Russell's homecoming from a distance. It was clear his wife was glad to see him back safe and sound, but Susanna's loss hung like a pall over the joy. And Sam McKee's claims were like a thorn in Ian's shoe.

Mary was terrified, he could see that. But her true needs were deeper than the land.

He pushed aside his desire to marry her.

Help me, Lord, help me to help her.

It was his prayer that night, and when he arose the next day to see to the animals, he whispered it again. He could only do what came to hand, do his duty, until the Lord saw fit to answer.

Checking on the sheep in the pen, their fleece moist with dew, he remembered the Lord's own kindness to him and took hope in that.

The great Shepherd was good. And He was able.

When it was time to go to the courthouse, Mary emerged from the house. Her glistening dark hair was carefully combed and pinned, her apron was neatly tied, and there was a firm set to her mouth.

Iain harnessed the mules to the Russells' wagon, helped Mary onto the seat next to Mr. Russell, and climbed in the back. The road to Staunton seemed long. As the wheels of the wagon rattled over the bridge just before town, Iain struggled with what to say to McKee's brother. He decided to simply be silent. The paperwork was indisputable, and John Russell was well respected.

Russell turned the mules onto Main Street, and Iain spotted a bay gelding tied in front of the courthouse. The scum had arrived already. His fists curled. Then he took a deep breath, forcing himself to be calm.

They went inside, Iain careful to remain slightly behind Mary. Not that she was in any danger.

"Ho, Captain Preston!" Russell greeted. One side of the courthouse was arranged with chairs and benches in a semicircle before an elevated cushioned chair. The judge's seat, presumably. The other was cluttered with boxes and chests. Here William Preston sat behind a trestle table smoking a pipe. Sam McKee stood to one side, arms crossed.

"Howdy," Preston responded, gesturing a welcome with his pipe. "How may I help ye?"

The former sheriff's nephew still possessed the fresh glow of youth, his blond good looks undisguised even in the dimly lit room. But he was not the sheriff. Another relative had taken that mantle in the last election.

Sam McKee placed a hand on the table. "I've come for justice. For my land."

Preston's eyebrows rose. "Russell?"

"The land in question is the indenture bounty of this woman. Her son owns the other piece in dispute."

Preston stood. "Names?"

John Russell gave their names and Preston, lodging the pipe in the corner of his mouth, squatted before the chests and opened one.

Mary's bosom rose and fell quickly, and her hands clenched into fists.

"Here we are. Mary Pickens and Thomas Pickens McKee. Seems in order." Preston's blue gaze flickered to Sam McKee, and Iain decided that Preston's acute judgment was merely disguised by a careless manner. He was a militia captain and an Indian fighter, after all.

McKee crossed his arms. "Simon McKee was my brother."

A faint expression crossed Preston's face that Iain could not fully read. Was he amused?

"Simon McKee never owned land in Augusta County." Preston gestured to the chests. "You might speak to my cousin, the sheriff, but I—"

"Simon married this wench to cover her shame. She's a—"

The next words sealed the man's fate. Iain stepped forward and swung. His fist met Sam McKee's jaw.

McKee stumbled back and tripped over a stool. Scrambling to his feet, he shouted, "I'll get you for this. That's assault!"

McKee's fists were tight, and his expression thunderous. John Russell's presence was solid and silent behind Ian.

The look on Preston's face flickered between amusement and seriousness. "McKee, you might face charges of disrupting the peace and slander."

Russell spoke. "Bringing shame on a woman's name is not a thing ye ought to do in this valley."

His words, clearly and solemnly spoken, hung in the air. Sam McKee looked at all of them in turn and fled.

Russell sighed. "And good riddance."

Iain's hand ached. He flexed it. "I'm sorry, Captain, for disturbing the court."

Preston smirked. "He had it coming."

Mary turned to him and smiled, her eyes shining with tears.

His heart warmed. But he dared not hope.

CHAPTER 20

$\mathcal{T}$he weather turned, the air brisk off the slopes. Maggie McClure was worried.

"The babe is crossways," she said one day while visiting. Mary went for a stool for her to sit down. The midwife had examined Mrs. Russell, and the line between her brows had deepened.

Mrs. Russell looked calm. "Shall we turn it?"

Mary suspected Mrs. Russell knew exactly what Maggie meant, as she was a midwife too. Probably had turned babes herself.

Maggie pursed her lips. "Let me take another look." Her knobby hands palpated Mrs. Russell's abdomen, along the line where her apron kept sliding up above her waist. "I think the babe lies face down, so that's a good thing. We may be able to coax the wee lad into position without much trouble."

Abigail Russell smiled. "You think it's a boy?"

"Just a hunch. Relax now." Maggie pressed her hands against Mrs. Russell's belly.

Mary's shoulders tensed. "May I help?" Their casual attitude did not fool her. Women died when something like this happened.

Neither answered her question. Mary dashed out the door with the buckets. Childbirth always required plenty of hot water. Labor had not started, but it could be any time, and it was something to do.

When she returned, Mrs. Russell was in the parlor in a strange position, on her hands and knees. Mary heated a kettle full of water. There was plenty of wood. That was good.

She thrust a splint of wood into the fire and went back to the parlor, where the midwife continued her ministrations. "Could be a while," Maggie said, looking up.

Mary took up a rag and cleaned.

And cleaned some more.

Finally she checked the parlor again. Mrs. Russell was sitting up, Maggie's hands on her belly.

Mrs. Russell looked at Mary as if to greet her, then a strange expression came over her face. "I-I think he's turning." She stood and placed her hands on her belly. "And..."

Mary knew that look. She glanced at the hearth. The fire was still blazing brightly. "I'll mind the children." She dashed outside and turned toward the stream. It was a favorite playing place. She'd take them up to Mrs. May's cabin. And Mrs. May would want to know Mrs. Russell was in labor.

As she strode briskly along the path her muscles relaxed. Surely Mrs. Russell would be safe. Maggie would see to it.

Tommy, Nathan, and Jonathan were fishing, their cane poles bobbing parallel above the water. Hannah and Joanie were playing in the mud, kneading brown oozing pretend dough. What a mess.

Tommy caught sight of her, and his face crunched in distress.

"No, you can stay here." Fishing would keep him out of trouble. "Hannah, Joanie, let's go up to Mrs. May's and feed the chickens."

The girls obeyed willingly enough, washing off the worst of the muddy streaks in the water, and they set off for the cabin.

According to Iain, the danger from the Shawnee was past. Last week the dried corn had been husked and braided to hang in the barn. The men were talking about the best places to hunt. Life had gone back to normal, except for the intensity of the evening prayers. Sometimes Mary trembled at Mr. Russell's groanings while wrestling with his Maker.

"I'll bless Thy Name even so, as Job did, but I'll never say I like it," he'd cried one night. "Return my daughter to me, for I ken well that Thou canst."

Over the weeks that followed, the prayers had been tempered by a solemn resignation that troubled Mary in a different way. Was Susanna already dead? Would they never see her again?

It seemed very possible, even probable.

Mrs. Russell's grief was quieter. A tear, a sigh, a sudden halt in her duties. Lately, though, her grief had been replaced by an inward contemplation. Hopefully her labor would be quick.

"Mrs. May!" Mary called as they approached the Mays' cabin, scattering chickens to either side.

"Mary?" Agnes May popped her head out the door. "Come ben. I have jam."

"Mrs. Russell is in labor. Maggie's here."

Mrs. May's brows drew together as she processed this. "Children, let's have some jam on bread." She reached for her cloak, grabbed a crock of herbs off a shelf, and left.

As it happened, the labor was quick. By the time the men came in from the fields, Mrs. May was back.

"A bonny wee laddie! Looks like his da, he does."

"I made porridge," Mary said. Her cooking was uninspired at best, but it was edible.

"I'll feed the menfolk here. Take a few bowls down for Abigail and Maggie."

It was dusk by the time she got to the house and tapped on the oak door.

Maggie opened it.

"What's his name?" Mary asked.

Maggie wouldn't say, but took the food and placed it on the table. "Go ask his mother."

Abigail Russell was lying in the parlor on a pallet bed, propped with a bolster. Tucked in one arm was a bundle of swaddling. Mary knelt.

Mrs. Russell's face was a little pale but otherwise she looked good. "Want to hold him?"

Mary took the bundle and her heart throbbed. In that moment she wanted another child, but pushed the thought away. It was impossible. "What's his name?"

"William. My father's name."

"Welcome to the world, William."

The child blinked up at her and she smiled. Then she looked at his mother. Mrs. Russell was asleep. Mary carefully placed the infant in the walnut cradle next to the bed and returned to the kitchen.

"She's sleeping."

"Come," Maggie indicated the bowls. "Come eat."

Mary apologized for the food while they ate.

"Nay. Just needs a little more salt and some basil. Abigail always has basil growing."

Mary placed the empty bowls in the basin to soak while Maggie thrust another few sticks into the fire.

"What's keeping you back, Mary?"

"What do you mean?"

"You need a husband and more bairns of your own."

Mary's neck felt warm. She must be blushing. "I-I—"

"I ken all about that last husband of yours. But that's no reason."

Iain's face came to mind. "I don't need to marry."

"The Bible says that it's not good for man to be alone. I ken it doesna say anything about a woman. But here in the valley I think it best that a woman not be alone. The nights can get awfully cold."

Mary sat back down and looked at Maggie McClure's lined face. Iain was kind. It wasn't that big a risk, was it? But she still wasn't good enough for him.

"I'll think about it, Mrs. McClure."

"Call me Maggie, lass."

Yes, she would think about it. Maybe she'd ask for a sign. Yes, that was it. She'd ask for a sign.

* * *

IAIN STEPPED over the threshold of the warm house gratefully. The first two days of the hunting trip had yielded nothing, but on the third day Mr. Russell brought down a fine buck. It was Jonathan's first season, and the lad killed a turkey the next day, to his great joy. Iain himself scored the biggest prize, a young elk. It took a full day to skin it, butcher the meat, and hang it in the smokehouse.

The kitchen was cheery with the scent of mulled cider and the sound of laughter. The laughter warmed his heart more than anything. His fatigue fell away. Joy had been missing from Russell's Ridge for so long.

Mrs. May welcomed them inside, clucking over the state of their clothing. "Look at the mud on your shoes! Knock off the worse of it here."

Iain used the iron boot scraper, a humble evidence of civilization and womankind everywhere. He needed one for his cabin. Whether or not Mary insisted, she deserved the little things, the small comforts.

If she would have him.

Mrs. Russell sat in the corner, her pink-cheeked babe chewing on his fist. Mr. Russell displayed Jonathan's turkey to the gathering while his son suddenly became shy.

"We need hot water for that," Mrs. May pronounced. "Feathers will come right off."

Iain had just divested himself of his jacket when Mary slipped past him and out the door, presumably to fetch more water. She wasn't wearing her cloak. He spotted the green-and-blue garment on its peg, grabbed it, and followed her quietly out the door.

The air was biting, especially after feeling the kitchen's warmth, but his trade shirt would keep him well enough. Mary's clothing was inadequate. He took the path to the spring and soon caught up to her.

"Mary?" Iain fumbled at his mistake. "Mrs. McKee?" He thought of her as Mary, but it still felt improper to use her Christian name.

A bucket dangling from her hand, she turned, a question in her eyes.

"I've your cloak. Ye forgot it."

"I-I was just fetching water."

A chill breeze swirled between them and swept gold-spangled leaves over the path. Iain stepped forward and swung the sturdy blue-and-green wool around her shoulders.

"Ye're cold." He had difficulty speaking. "And there's nae rush."

Mary grabbed one edge of the cloak with one hand while the other remained curled firmly around the bucket's handle. The loose edge of the garment flapped in the breeze. "But—"

"Mary, ye're no' a servant." He reached around her shoulder and pulled the cloak closely around her. "And if ye'll have me, I'd like to be your husband."

* * *

MARY SIMPLY GAPED at him for a long moment. She knew of his interest, but still it surprised her that he'd ask.

"But-but—"

"I'll no' harm ye."

She took a deep breath. She was grateful for his kindness. How to explain? "You're a good man, Iain MacLeod. You deserve a good woman."

There. It was said.

Ian blinked, as if confused, then understanding washed over his face. Perhaps he'd be able to look elsewhere now. He said nothing at first, merely taking the bucket handle from her fingers.

"There is none of us good," he said. "'There is none righteous, no, not one.'"

That was in the Bible. They were all sinners, it was true. "But some sins—"

"Maybe. But do ye wish to sin? To keep on doing what ye ken is wrong?"

Mary opened her mouth but had nothing to say. Of course, she didn't wish to sin. Had she sinned with Mr. Byrd?

The Bordens would have said it was his fault, she was sure, and yet, she had always felt a vague guilt. It was shameful to have a child out of wedlock. But she had never desired the situation.

No, of course not. She would never in a million years allow Mr. Byrd to touch her again.

"Besides." Iain tugged her cloak more tightly about her. "Our sins are washed by the blood of Christ, and His righteousness is ours."

The cloak. The warm wool about her shoulders. Mrs. Borden's words about Jesus' robe of righteousness.

Was it a sign? Somehow it didn't matter, because the truth of those words fell upon her and seemed real for the very first time.

His righteousness is ours.

Ian reached into his clothing and pulled out a glittering object. He pulled the cloak together and fastened it. "Got this in trade."

It was beautiful. A Scottish brooch. Tears poured down her face.

"What did I do? Do ye not care for it?"

"No, Iain, it's wonderful. But the cloak—Mrs. Borden explained to me about Jesus' righteousness. But I don't think I believed it until now."

Her throat swelled and she couldn't say another word. But a peace descended on her and joy filled her heart.

CHAPTER 21

*M*ary followed Iain and Mr. Russell into the courthouse. Her heart began to pound.

Behind the counter stood Captain Preston and the sheriff. A piece of paper lay on a rough counter before them. The marriage license, nestled between a stoneware inkwell and several sharpened quills.

Mary clenched her hands. Her palms were sweating despite the December chill. Did she really want to marry this man?

Iain's jaw was clean, carefully shaved early this morning, no doubt. A smile played upon his lips. He adjusted his jacket, then sneaked a glance at her.

A happy glance.

She smiled back, and her whole body seemed to relax. Yes, she did want to marry him.

A shadow fell over the doorway.

"Dinna say we're late!" A familiar voice.

Mary turned. Mrs. Borden and her new husband entered the room.

"G'day, John, Mrs. Bowyer," Mr. Russell said.

Bowyer. Mrs. Bowyer now. But she looked the same, a woman of mature beauty—and a kind nature. And her cloak matched Mary's own. The Campbell tartan.

The story connected to the cloak swept over her yet again, the weight of the wool on her shoulders a reminder that *yes, her shame was covered. Totally covered.*

Mrs. Bowyer stepped next to Mary, eyes twinkling. "I would not miss this for the world."

There was no ceremony except for a heartfelt prayer offered by Mr. Russell. More of the Russells would be here, but the real celebration would be at home, and all the women were cooking. The savory smells had begun to rise even before they left for Staunton.

Captain Preston pushed the license toward her, and Mary signed her name. The action echoed the previous vows she'd made with quill and ink. The first signature, on her indenture contract, meant years of servanthood. The second, her first marriage, meant the same, another kind of bondage.

This time was different.

Iain was different.

She was different.

She was a freewoman now. A freewoman in truth. Free in Christ, like the minister said.

So then, brethren, we are not children of the bondwoman, but of the free.

The promises of God were a free gift. She still struggled with the idea sometimes. Other times it was as clear as mountain sunshine. *Grace.* Grace was free.

And Christ Jesus came for sinners.

She blinked away the moisture that sprang to her eyes. She was free, and so was Iain. And she had nothing to fear from him.

Iain signed, and the witnesses stepped forward, first Mrs. Bowyer, then Mr. Russell, who signed his name with a flourish.

"Congratulations," Captain Preston said, smiling. "You are man and wife. Are we invited to the ceilidh?"

* * *

THERE WAS NO DANCING. Somehow Susanna's absence—not to mention the chilly weather—seemed to preclude a valley-wide frolic. But Thomas Kerr had brought a large jug of what Iain suspected was Cunningham's brew. Two-year old whiskey, most probably.

It was hog butchering time, and one of the Russell pigs now turned on a spit over the fire pit Mary used for laundry, releasing a tantalizing aroma. A roast goose sat on one of the trestle tables in the parlor, surrounded by pies of every description, among other things.

The children's faces were already marked with crumbs from scones and tarts, but Mrs. May's scolding sounded half-hearted.

He no longer heard her voice—where was she now? He had so much to thank her for.

Finally, Iain spotted Mrs. May coming down the path from her cabin—and his. She caught his eye. "Now at least ye'll have a place to sleep—and two pillows!"

A confused mixture of embarrassment and thankfulness washed over him. "Thank ye kindly," he sputtered. Agnes May was right, as always. His wife couldn't sleep on his rough pallet. He wondered what he'd find in its place.

Mary came up to stand beside him, and Mrs. May looped her arms around her. "Iain's become like my own son. And now I have a daughter."

Iain's chest tightened as he fought tears. Mary wiped her eyes, and Mrs. May clucked. "I need to see to the currant cake." Mrs. May left.

The jangle of harness sounded from below. A late comer. The Bowyers' carriage drew near Grandda's cabin and jerked to a halt. Iain spotted Samuel McClure helping his wife Maggie down from the carriage. John Bowyer jumped from the seat and saw to the horses while Mrs. Bowyer appeared in the carriage door.

"Am I late? Everything smells wonderful. I went to the McClures' shop after the signing and brought them both."

Iain bowed to her. "Just in time."

"Iain," Mrs. Bowyer said. "I have heard ye're good with horses. I've a wedding gift. One of Dobbie's get."

John Bowyer drew near leading a dark bay horse. Very young, with alert ears and clear dark eyes.

"Nimrod will be a two-year-old in the spring."

Iain traced the lines of the horse with his eyes, marveling. "But-but—"

"No buts," Mrs. Bowyer said. "We have enough to do without training a stubborn colt."

Iain took the lead rope from her husband's hand. "This is incredibly generous."

Mrs. Bowyer harrumphed. "Mr. Borden died and left me rich. I can do as I like"—she smiled at her husband—"within reason, or so he says."

Iain caught John Bowyer's eye, but the man shrugged and smiled.

"Mary, think we can adopt this creature?"

"He's beautiful."

Iain almost wept.

Mary was his wife. And not only that, he now had the

start of a stable. Something he'd never actually wished for, not consciously. Only rich men bred horses.

But maybe in this new land he'd breed them too.

EPILOGUE

SIX YEARS LATER

*M*ary MacLeod touched the new window's glass. She'd cleaned it just yesterday, and she could see all the way to the road winding next to the South River. Iain had chosen a good place for the new house, atop a rolling rise that commanded a view of much of their property. Her land was to her right, shielded from view by the line of cottonwoods along the stream. Her land, that had produced the madder root that had paid for this window.

Their land. It was all their land, really. And though Iain had said little when she'd voiced the desire to pay for something herself, the reality was that it no longer felt as important as it once had, to have an income of her own.

It was simply part of God's provision. The madder, the sheep, and soon—Ian hoped—a new colt. His stable now consisted of Nimrod and two mares, one of them great with foal.

She ran her hand over her swollen belly with joy. Iain had consented to naming the new babe after himself after only a brief argument.

"I'm too young to be called Auld Iain."

"Andrew Lewis calls you 'Mac,' and the rest call you MacLeod. I'm the only one who might, and you're not old to my eyes."

Then conversation had ceased.

She surveyed the meadow outside and caught sight of her husband. Iai n was checking on the Robinson lad, who served as an under-shepherd of sorts. The fellow was learning. But the ram tended to push him around.

What would she call the babe if it were a girl? The name Archibald had been an easy choice for the first child who came along, and then when the second proved a girl, they named her after Iain's mother, Jane.

Mary needed another name. Abigail? Agnes?

Magdalena? Yes. Magdalena Bowyer had proved a friend indeed. She would name a daughter after her.

Suddenly the door popped open, followed by her firstborn.

"Thomas Pickens MacLeod!" It still felt wonderful to call him by Iain's name. It had been Tommy's own idea, not even a year after their marriage. To have the last name of a rumored Jacobite was attractive in a dark kind of way, rather like being called a pirate by other children. Whereas the name McKee was universally despised. Besides, Iain was the only true father Tommy really remembered.

It was good and right.

"Visitors!" Tommy's voice cracked, the pitch jumping high. Nathan Russell's voice had already changed, and Jonathan was six feet tall but still growing.

"I didn't see anyone on the road." Had they come over the Gap?

He shrugged, then ran out the door again, dark hair coming loose from its binding.

She rose and reached for her favorite bowl. It would be easy enough to stir up the ingredients for cornbread and set it to bake before she walked up to the house.

Company meant more folks to feed, and one couldn't have too much cornbread.

Visitors. From Richmond, to the east? Or—

The letters from Shawnee country were sparse, carried by Indian traders or mountain men, but the last one had hinted at a visit. Could it be?

* * *

THE DOG BARKED, and Iain turned toward the sound. A three-legged fox hound followed Joanie and young Arch everywhere; it barked at foxes, keeping them away from the chickens, and announced visitors. Had someone come to Russell's Ridge?

He turned back. The sheep were chewing contentedly, the muzzles working busily sideways, masticating the rich late-spring grass. The dog barked again, and skinny Sam Robinson glanced in the direction of the noise.

"Lad, I'll be up to the house." On the Ridge the "house" still meant the Russells'. Iain and Mary's new house was not quite as grand, though it had a roomy loft for children, a necessity now. The old cabin had been converted to a lambing shed two years ago.

"What about Maisie?"

One of the ewes had yet to lamb. Her sides were big, curved like a whiskey keg. She was carrying twins. At least.

"She'll be fine. I'll put her in the shed tonight. Not that she needs it." The lambing shed was mainly necessary for early births as a spring night could get cold. But the days were warm, and the nights mild.

He started for the house but was only halfway there when he heard Agnes May scream.

He ran. Ahead, the clearing was thronged with people. Mrs. May was embracing a tall woman.

The woman had dark hair and wore a familiar red skirt.

It was Susanna.

* * *

MARY COULDN'T SEE what was causing the commotion as she strode along. Iain's form came into view through the trees. He was standing on the edge of the clearing in front of the Russells' home.

She came alongside him and caught her breath. A man and woman—his hair light, hers dark, even darker than her father's. Jamie Paxton and Susanna. Jamie held a toddler in his arms, and a little girl clung to Susanna's skirts.

Probably terrified, poor thing.

Jamie had gone to preach to the Shawnee and stumbled upon the Indians holding Susanna captive. She'd known enough of the language to translate for him, and some of the Shawnee had embraced Christ.

They were married now.

Letters had filtered back, carried by Indian traders. Letters full of good news. Children, both physical and spiritual.

Mary slipped her hand into Iain's.

"They're back," he said.

"For good?"

"I dinna ken."

She threaded her fingers through his. "I think I understand now."

"Hmm?"

"God can use even the darkest things for good."

Susanna's capture. Her own troubles.

Iain looked at her but said nothing for a moment. When he spoke, his voice was low and husky. *"Ach leanaidh maith is tròcair rium, an cian a bhios mi beò; is còmhnaicheam an àros Dhè, ri fad mo rè 's mo lò."*

She recognized the verse. "'Surely goodness—'"

"'And lovingkindness—'"

"'Shall follow me.'" She laid her head on his shoulder.

God was good.

Thank you for reading this story! If you liked it, please leave a rating or write a short review on Amazon, Goodreads, or Bookbub. Feedback is a great encouragement to authors and it helps potential readers too!

For writing news and discounts, sign up for my newsletter.

If you are interested in Jamie and Susanna's story, check out *The Heart of Courage.* Keep reading for an excerpt from book three in the series, *A Fallen Sparrow: A Novel of the American Revolution.*

* * *

Catholics had a hard time of it in the American colonies. Every year on November 5th, Guy Fawkes day in Britain, colonists in Boston celebrated the capture of Catholic assassins who attempted to kill (Protestant) James I in 1605. They had a parade complete with costumes and burned the Pope in effigy.

It wasn't a mere prejudice or hatred of Catholic people. Americans in the 1700s still remembered the horrors of the 1500s. Protestants were burned at the stake by Queen Mary. Then they were persecuted by King Charles I, who declared that anything he did was right because God had appointed him (the "divine right" of kings). These last troubles sent Christians across the ocean to settle New England.

They hadn't forgotten why they had fled England. Most in the colonies could read, and owned the Bible, *Foxe's Book of Martyrs*, and perhaps *The Pilgrim's Progress.* Foxe's book compiles accounts of believers who lost their lives for their faith, and John Bunyan wrote his famous allegory in a prison, one of those persecuted under Charles II.

To the average Christian in the colonies, there were two

aspects of Catholicism to fear: first was doctrinal. Justification by faith was the clarion call of the Reformation, and ministers in the 1600s and during the Great Awakening returned to it frequently, fearing the "papist" doctrine of salvation by works.

The second was political. Up until the Revolutionary War time period, church and state were not separate. Catholic states (like France) were feared, because what if they conquered the colonies? Freedom to worship God according to the Scriptures would be lost or at least made terribly difficult.

Maryland was settled as a safe haven for Catholics as they in turn began to suffer persecution under Protestant regimes. But it was not until Congress and the states ratified the First Amendment did true religious liberty come to our nation.

What a blessed heritage we have!

* * *

Magdalena (Woods) McDowell Borden Bowyer was a real woman. She was (literally) a colorful person, living in a red house, riding a black horse, and wearing a green cloak. Her first husband was killed in an Indian skirmish. A "pillar" in the church, she next married a Quaker, Benjamin Borden, who consented to attending the Presbyterian meetinghouse near their home in modern-day Rockbridge County. Smallpox brought grief to their family. Benjamin died, as well as two small children, Hannah and Elizabeth. For story purposes I just mentioned Elizabeth.

Within the year she remarried. John Bowyer was younger than she and had served as the Bordens' steward or manager. By all accounts Magdalena was vivacious and intelligent—

and beautiful. Perhaps she was a little eccentric as well. One particular stood out to me—the green cloak. The other things were certainly notable—riding a black charger around —but green was an ordinary color in the 18th century. It was common for middle-class or wealthy individuals to wear colorful clothing.

Then I remembered that she was a Campbell through her mother. And not an ordinary Campbell. She was a relation of the laird of the clan, The Earl of Argyll. I looked up the tartan colors of the Campbells. Blue and green. From afar this might be seen—or remembered—as "green."

Perhaps we'll never know for sure. But it was fun to write about her.

Indentured servitude was common in the 18th century, especially as a way for impoverished folks from Northern Ireland to emigrate. It was not the same as slavery, but is it easy to imagine how it could be oppressive. The length of the contract varied from four to six years (at least seven for prisoners), and by law masters had to send their servants away at the end of their contracts with tools of their trade or some other means of support. So when John Russell gifts Ian MacLeod with a bit of land and some sheep, it was not out of the ordinary (though he was a generous person). The fifty acres was guaranteed to all indentures in Virginia.

There were several Jacobite rebellions in Scotland during the 18th century. The choice of George of Hanover as the next king after the death of Queen Anne was controversial, and not just among Catholic Scots. Anne's half-brother James was passed over in favor of a German cousin who did not even speak English. But the motive had to do with religion. Many in Britain did not want a Catholic king. George was safely Protestant.

In the first book in the Russells series, *The Shenandoah*

Road, we learn that the (fictional) character Arch May's father fought (and was killed) at Sheriffmuir. This was a battle during the first Jacobite uprising in 1715 ("Jacobite" derives from the Latin for "James"). The second uprising, 1745-46, coalesced around the "Bonnie Prince" Charles, James's son, who led the rebel army. It failed spectacularly at Culloden. Afterward, the Duke of Cumberland's men ravaged the Scottish countryside, killing and burning. Important leaders were drawn and quartered in London, and Parliament passed an act forbidding the wear of the clan tartans, among other things.

Prisoners were often sent to the colonies. Many ended up in North Carolina, but not all. I had fun thinking of places where Ian might have ended up. The Belvoir plantation is real; so is Belmont, where Eliza Pinckney famously worked out a way to make indigo prosper in the American South. It eventually became a major cash crop.

Malaria was endemic to the South in those days. Many famous people, including General Sam Houston of Texas, suffered from malaria at some point. Spread by mosquitoes in warm and wet areas, it afflicted many of the indentured servants. Contracting some sort of illness was expected and was known as "seasoning."

Sadly, the Byrd family is quite real. I imagined William Byrd's behavior based on his father's. The man kept a diary that was very revealing. Certainly the position of a servant in a household like that would have been a fraught one. Mary's feelings are confused. She feels guilty because she thinks she should have resisted her master's advances more. This is a difficult subject to write about because not all rape or sexual abuse is as cut and dried as we might think. It wasn't in Mary's case. I would like to tell her, "Don't feel guilty, it wasn't your fault." But I wrote a different solution for Mary. Tell me what you think!

* * *

You may have noticed some unfamiliar words in this story. For example, Ian speak Gaelic and knew bits of the Gaelic psalter. In Scotland, and to a lesser extent in Northern Ireland, Scottish Gaelic was spoken by many up until about this time in history. During the 19th century, it was spoken less and less, and it disappeared in some places. Today, efforts are being made to revitalize and reintroduce this unique language, which has no close linguistic relationship to English.

Words like "kailyard" (literally, kale yard, meaning garden) and idioms like "Come ben" (Come inside, a form of welcome) are not Gaelic. They are Scots English, which is said by some to be a separate language from British (or American) English. Certainly, much of Scots vocabulary and idioms are unique to the dialect, and an American would be helpless listening to it. Go to Scotland today and you will hear a mixture of British English with a local accent, Scots English, and possibly even Gaelic, depending on where you are.

The minister in our story, a real life man from Antrim, John Craig, preached sermons in British English. But when speaking of the difficulty of finding elders to appoint in churches on the frontier, he said when he couldn't find a stone, he'd use a dornach, a Gaelic word for pebbly spot.

One reason American English differs from British English is because of immigrants. The Scots and Scots-Irish flooded into the country in the 18th century, and some words we think of as quite ordinary are actually Scots words:

malarkey and smidgen are two of them. In certain areas, like the Appalachians, things get interesting. In the hills, a "poke" is a bag. That's Scots in origin.

And Nashville? Listen to Celtic ballads, and you'll make the connection.

* * *

Excerpt from the Russells Book 3, *A Fallen Sparrow: A Novel of the American Revolution:*

* * *

Let me observe, how fatal are the effects, of posting a standing army among a free people!
—Samuel Adams, December 10, 1770

JULY 1771

The sun beat down on the back of his regimental uniform as Lieutenant Robert Shirley approached Ashby Castle, his mare trotting smoothly beneath him despite the long hours on the road. She had proven to be a good mount, worth every penny he'd paid Richard Tattersall.

Leicestershire was square in the middle of nowhere, but it was a beautiful nowhere. Lambs gamboled near their dams on green rolling hills; stands of oak and beech marked gurgling streams. It was the place of his youth. And it was the Shirley family seat, and no matter how the Shirleys might be whispered about in London, this place was still home.

His godmother had summoned him, and he had no idea why. Especially since his commanding officer had given him extended leave as a result. It was unheard of. The Countess of Huntingdon had a certain fame, but only in religious circles. How she could influence a colonel he had no clue.

The castle ruins loomed before him, and Robert guided his horse around the skeleton of the tower, slowing her to a walk. Beside his commission, the mare was the only property he had left; he would not push her past her limits.

Ashby Place came into view, a picturesque manor, the only part of the estate that had been maintained—and that just barely. Ivy crawled over weathered gray stone, and several rose bushes extended unpruned branches in riotous color.

A groom emerged from the stable. Robert dismounted and entrusted the mare to the young man before climbing the steps. He employed the iron knocker, but almost before he'd finished Grayson opened the door.

The butler looked the same every time he came, though today, as Robert followed the man through the hall, the butler's gait seemed slower than before, his stride more halting.

Robert glanced to the left, where a double door opened upon a large drawing room.

It was empty, which seemed strangely incongruous. The last time he'd been there, three years before, Mr. Whitefield had preached to a packed room.

The preacher's strange squinty eyes and humble dress had faded away before the dramatic force of his words. Standing against the wall listening, Robert began to understand the drawing power of the minister. And he believed the claims of thousands gathering in open fields to hear him speak.

But the magnetic voice left no lasting impression. Robert had been baptized in the Church of England and attended services occasionally, as all gentlemen did. That was

certainly sufficient for his soul, though if others were bene-
fited by this man's preaching, he welcomed it.

Grayson led him to the back parlor. Sunlight filtered in
from a large window framed by aging green drapes; the
familiar furnishings were worn but tasteful. A man sat with
the countess, a tea table between them. The man wore no
wig but his cravat was fine and edged with lace. Robert stiff-
ened to attention as the butler announced him.

"Come join us, Robert." His godmother's angular face
retained a mature beauty, like the charm of the manor itself,
ancient and settled. She addressed her companion. "Lord
Dartmouth, may I present my godson, who is also a relation
on my mother's side. Lieutenant Robert Shirley, the Earl of
Dartmouth."

The man's dress, subdued in color but expensive, had
already signaled his rank. Robert bowed. "I am honored."

The Earl of Dartmouth possessed warm hazel eyes and a
lively mouth. "The biscuits are quite good."

He'd heard of this man, a staunch Methodist. Once he'd
heard the moniker Psalm Singer applied to him in mockery.

"Sit, Robert."

He perched on a faded settee and waited while the
countess poured him tea, wondering again why he'd been
summoned. His neck was abominably hot underneath his
military stock.

She handed him a cup and he took it carefully.

"Countess, what news from Georgia?" The earl asked.

They ignored Robert as he sipped his tea, strong Bohea.
They seemed to be discussing George Whitefield's
orphanage.

"The new caretakers have arrived," the countess said.

Listening, Robert gathered that Whitefield's orphanage
had been left in his godmother's care. Not a surprise—she'd

supported the minister financially while he lived. It seemed her religious work continued after the man's death, both across the Atlantic and in various other places, including a college for ministers. He focused on the tea tray, where biscuits crowded pastries and scones.

His stomach rumbled.

His godmother's dark gaze shifted to him. "Eat, Robert."

"My lady." He snagged a scone and nibbled at it. The house might look neglected, but his godmother had a fine cook. The flaky treat melted in his mouth, a far cry from anything the army had to offer.

He was on a second cup of tea when the conversation turned to him.

"Robert, Lord Dartmouth has a proposal for you."

"My lord?" He hoped he had no crumbs on his face.

Dartmouth put down his cup with a clink. "You have no doubt heard of the unrest in the colonies. And most recently, the unfortunate incident in Boston."

Robert replaced his cup. "The officers of my regiment took note of Captain Preston's situation." The earl's open expression encouraged him to continue. "Of course there was great sympathy, and some confusion over the legalities."

"Oh?"

"The colonel of my regiment said the man ought to have been tried by a military court." Robert said.

"The colonel is right. Of course, there were political realities to consider," the earl said.

Robert wasn't sure why this was important. In London, unrest was periodically put down, a few lives always lost in the process. Regrettable, but it was life. Peace and order must be maintained. In any case, no harm was done—the Boston court had cleared Preston of murder.

Robert studied the earl's face, remembering that he was

Lord North's stepbrother. And a very important man in his own right—he held some kind of ministry post. Why would he take note of a mere lieutenant?

"Political realities are important," the earl continued. "We erred by passing the Stamp Act when we had no idea of how it would affect the common man."

Robert frowned. The citizens of Great Britain were routinely taxed; why the colonies refused a small contribution was beyond him. "My lord."

"I began to cultivate sources of information beside the usual channels. A sea captain, for instance, has regularly supplied me with intelligence."

Intelligence. Belly tensing, Robert nodded in response.

"Your godmother trusts you, and that is why we have summoned you today. You would report only to me."

"My lord—but—"

""I have contacted your commanding officer. Your commission is now inactive. You are no longer under oath until such time as we deem it best to reinstate you."

We deem it best …He had no choice. "A spy? I will spy for you?" It was horrifying. Spying was dirty work. He was a gentleman. Granted, he had no title, but still.

The man's hazel gaze turned no-nonsense and penetrating. "We are not at war with a foreign power. Our troops merely keep the King's peace." The earl reached for a pastry. "Therefore, you will not be a spy, only an observer. Still, there are several reasons for removing you from active duty." He took a bite, chewed, and swallowed. "For one thing, you will be able to move about without suspicion. We may ask for information leading to the arrest of a ringleader. If you are able to insert yourself into their number, all the better."

Robert's mind whirled. He was being ripped from his duty here with the Fifth Regiment and inserted into the melee of Boston political intrigue, a totally unknown world. The parlor itself seemed to waver. "But General Gage? Does he have his own sp—sources?"

Dartmouth paused while the countess handed him another cup of tea. "General Gage uses his own judgment. We have given him considerable leeway in his command. After all, we are three thousand miles away. But consider this, lieutenant. It is clear the inhabitants of Boston hate the soldiers stationed there. How is Gage to gather intelligence? How is he to discover the thinking of the ordinary man? Worse, he will have difficulties discovering the plots of the rebels."

Discovering the plots of the rebels. This was a serious task. He had only one more card to play, a weak one. "I have a cousin who might be willing to serve in this capacity."

Lord Dartmouth studied him.

His godmother arched an eyebrow. "Nonsense. Lord Rawdon is too young." Her voice dripped with what she would not say, that her grandson's character was deficient. Robert's cousin was a scapegrace and a follower of the rake-hell Banastre Tarleton. Both had been behind him several years at both Harrow and Oxford, and they were notorious for bullying the youngest students. Rawdon's father had washed his hands of him, and his uncle had purchased him a commission.

She was right. There was no escape. "My lord, I am honored to serve King and country."

"Your country thanks you," the earl said dryly, "even if the King remains ignorant of your service. Your godmother brings a quiet honor to the Shirley name—"

Of course the Earl of Dartmouth knew the ignominious elements of the family history. He'd been at the trial.

"—and you will receive a reward. You will receive your

officer's half pay plus a generous stipend. And,"—his face turned friendly again—"I hear you have a mare with good bloodlines."

Robert wrinkled his brow. Horses didn't do well on Atlantic crossings. "Yes, she is a sweet goer. Good disposition."

"Statecraft stands at stud in my stables. I'll house her, and if you wish, breed her while you're away."

Despite Dartmouth's religious interests and modest clothing, he was a wealthy man, and it would not surprise Robert if he bred blooded horses.

"I'd be honored, my lord. I won't need a mount?"

The earl's mouth twitched. "Perhaps, but men are judged by their horses, and your mare will shout that you are not a humble bookbinder."

Robert's mouth fell open. "Bookbinder?" Gentlemen did not labor with their hands.

His godmother had a twinkle in her eye. She knew?

"I have arranged it. A discreet master bookbinder at Longman and Sons will teach you the trade, and you'll be ready to depart for Boston early next year."

Robert blinked. "Yes, my lord." What else could he say?

ACKNOWLEDGMENTS

There are so many to thank. Pegg Thomas, an award-winning historical writer, gave me useful input on my draft. My critique partners likewise helped with goofball writing and stray—or missing—commas. Thanks go to Bob, Lynda, and Diane of Scribes 254, and Alynda, Kirsten, Judy, Teresa, and Dena of Word Weavers Page 24. I appreciate you all!

My sister, Susan, gave me helpful feedback as well. My first chapter is greatly improved as a result. What is in my head doesn't always make it onto the page, and I need someone to say, I don't get it.

Thanks to my proofreader, Trudy Cordle, and to my ARC readers. Can't do it without y'all.

A big thank you to my husband, who comes home to a woman peering at the computer. He's encouraged my writing efforts from the beginning.

And of course I give glory to the Lord, Who sustains us with every breath we take. May these stories honor Him in every way.

Soli Deo Gloria.

ALSO BY LYNNE BASHAM TAGAWA

The Russells:

The Shenandoah Road: A Novel of the Great Awakening

The Heart of Courage: A Novel of the French and Indian War

A Fallen Sparrow: A Novel of the American Revolution

Romantic Suspense:

A Twisted Strand

Nonfiction:

Sam Houston's Republic